Once Upon A Time....Papa

A Collection of 11 Short Stories

BY

DOMINIC F. CHUCK

ILLUSTRATED BY

ROGER FERREIRA

AGNEL PUBLISHING

AGNEL PUBLISHING TORONTO

National Library of Canada
Ottawa, Ontario Canada
ISBN 0-9698791-6-4

Editor in chief
Elton Adams

Illustrator & Cover Design
Roger Ferreira

Formatting and Computer Scanning
Megan Yhan

Reviewed
Anna Ganza

Back Cover Photography
Black's Studio (Stoney Creek, Ontario)

Printed by St. Joseph Printing
50 Macintosh Blvd.,
Concord, Ontario
Canada L4K 4P3

Published by AGNEL PUBLISHING

ACKNOWLEDGMENTS

The successful completion of any book requires assistance and input from several sources. Thus my eternal gratitude is extended to the following:

The guidance and inspiration of the Holy Spirit.

To my dear wife Sue for her continuing encouragement, suggestions and proofreading.

To my dear friend and editor-in-chief, Elton Adams for his meticulous editing of my manuscript, organizing of the material, and insightful suggestions and meaningful comments.

To my illustrator Roger Ferreira for his excellent pictorial illustrations.

To my dear daughter Megan for formatting, computer scanning, proofreading and valuable suggestions.

To dear Ana Ganza for book review, continued support and resourceful suggestions.

DEDICATION

These short stories have been lovingly dedicated to my dear grandchildren Samantha and Andrew and in a very special way to Alexandra. They are also dedicated in memory of my dear infant son Joseph Martin and my sister, Hilda.

NOTE FROM THE AUTHOR

The characters and the names in these Short Stories, except in the first story are fictional. Any mention of names, which may be synonymous to that of any person or animal is strictly coincidental and bears no relationship to anyone living or dead.

CONTENTS

FOREWORD

While growing up as a young boy in my native Trinidad, I had the privilege of reading and thoroughly enjoying Aesop's fables. These animal tales had a fascination and dynamism that attracted me to them, and at times I felt myself transported into their world, where I could clearly identify with one of the characters. Aesop's fables have left an indelible impression on me.

Each of his stories impelled the reader to think, to use valued judgment and to learn from the mistakes of others. The reader was sure to benefit from the moral lessons, which I have found useful throughout the years: and it is against this background that I have based my short stories.

My aim in writing and presenting these short stories is a deliberate attempt on my part to revitalize, rekindle and ignite interest in this art form, to stress essential qualities that we often take for granted, and to show the consequences of making false assumptions, or poor judgments.

We are living in a time so filled with contradictions, that any attempt to portray good values is misconstrued as misguided and preachy. I make no claims of being an authority on moral values, but at the same time, I make no apology for trying to explain my position on moral issues, as we all do need directions in our lives.

Thus my primary objective is to tell an interesting story - one that is designed to help the reader discover the beauty that lies in thoughtful actions. To show that selfishness, greed, false assumptions, pride, jealousy and self-pity do nothing positive to enhance a proper lifestyle, but they inevitably lead to a low self-esteem and sometimes to utter destruction of the individual.

In the eleven short stories, which I have presented to you my dear reader, I hope that I have accomplished that feat, and that you will find something of merit in them. I trust that both young children as well as adults will be able to enjoy this timely adventure.

INTRODUCTION

The eleven short stories have been divided into two groups for convenience.

Group 1 Short Stories (1-5) have been written primarily for children at the pre secondary school. These stories are introduced by short story 1, which is really intended for parents, teachers, group-leaders and adults. It provides an insight into why these stories can be an excellent motivator in helping to mould healthy minds that are more likely to favour the achievement of success in their later lives.

The stories themselves provide a framework for many group exercises that relate to character building. Several can even be used as bedtime stories, since they nourish the imagination. Others encourage the child to ask 'why?' or identify the motives behind actions. It is even possible to use a play format to properly and forcefully illustrate in a more dramatic fashion the essential elements in the story.

Group 2 Short Stories (6-11) continues from where Group 1 stories leave off. They provide an opportunity for adolescent children (11- young adults) to examine their own mind set, beliefs and inclinations.

These are really human stories that on close examination revel much about ourselves. In essence they invite us to examine our own habits of thought and action, which have, in many instances, become subconscious, habits of thought and action that hurt and sometimes permanently injure and sear both others and ourselves.

The stories are short, but without exception they encourage reflection. Hopefully they may bring about a change for the better in character formation and attitudes of the reader.

In addition, these stories can provide a healthy alternative to TV watching and can be used as the basis for enjoyable and instructive conversation at the dinner table, or in the classroom setting.

Elton Adams
Editor-in-chief

GROUP I
SHORT STORIES

ONE DAY ADVENTURE

SAMANTHA, ANDREW and PAPA

Grand children are precious in the eyes of God. They are interesting, loving but demanding of our attention. Young children are not only God's gift to us, but they are also a source of great joy and are generally blessed with boundless energy. Their fascination with Nature, and their capacity to imagine and inquire is limitless. One has only to take the time to listen to them. It is equally important to provide simple answers and solutions readily to their young, inquiring and developing minds. Meeting their observational needs with a simple explanation, is a priority, which when given, offers an avenue for learning.

In this true-life adventure story, an attempt is made to show how I did just that with my five year old granddaughter, Samantha and my four year old grandson, Andrew. It all happened one day, in the summer of '93, while vacationing with them at the Pine Isle Resort in Atlanta, USA.

It was late July. The day began stiflingly damp and hot with a very heavy, early morning downpour, which soon gave way to brilliant sunshine. It was a little after 10 a.m., and there was little else to do in the hotel at that time of the day, so I decided to take them on a little adventure walk.

Holding hands together, we trudged along, Samantha, Andrew and I. Here and there, we explored a broken twig, a fallen leaf, a discarded object, a bug, or anything that we chanced to meet on our way. For children, even the simplest of objects or life forms will arouse their curiosity. Children are naturally fascinated with our environment; and this fascination can give rise to great opportunities for learning.

Making our way along a narrow and gentle sloping path and holding hands, we strolled in single file, Samantha, Andrew and I.
"Oh, Papa, look. This seed has wings," said Samantha, as she fingered a small airborne seed.
"Papa, can it fly?" inquired little Andrew innocently.
"No bozo head!" Samantha shouted authoritatively.

"Please Samantha," I said rather sternly, "That's not a kind thing to say to your brother. Now, no silly name calling!"
"Sorry Andrew, "I really didn't mean it."
"Then you shouldn't have said it," I affirmed.

"Well, let's see whether it can fly, then we will be able to provide Andrew with the correct answer to his question. See Sammy, if we want to learn, or discover the truth, we must start by asking questions."
Actually there was no need to remind her of this, because Samantha just loves asking questions. We each tossed a seed in the air. They were instantly caught up in a passing breeze. They floated a while and fell but a short distance away.
"See, papa, see, they flew." They both shouted excitedly.
"Yes, papa, they can fly, eh papa? Mine flew papa," said Samantha.
"And mine too," chimed in Andrew.

"Yes, wind dispersed seeds, they're air-borne seeds," I explained.
"And what's that papa?" inquired Samantha.
"Well," I said, "God has provided them with little projections, shaped like little wings. He also made them light, so they can be carried by the wind, when they fall off the tree."
"They float like feathers because they are light, eh papa?"

"Yes, Samantha, like feathers. Their little wings allow them to be borne by the wind, or air and so they are said to be air borne."
"That's neat eh papa?"
"Yes, Sammy, very neat."

I continued, "You see, in this way, they have a better chance to survive and germinate into a young plant.
"What is to germinate, Papa?"
"It means to start growing."
"You mean like us."
"Yes, Sammy, like you and Andrew, except that you both started growing a long time ago in your mother's womb."

Continuing, I explained to them that if the seeds all fell under the tree and they all germinated, there would be over crowding. The young plants will not get sufficient sunshine and many will die. Those that survive a longer time will remain weak and sickly, because they need adequate space to thrive well, so they too may eventually die."

"Yes, Papa, but what about fruit trees, like Andrew's plum tree, or my apple tree? Papa, some of the ripe fruits fall on the ground under the tree," observed Samantha.
Indeed in my backyard, I have told Andrew that the plum tree is his, and the apple tree is Samantha's. She has seen apples strewn on the ground beneath her tree, but she had never asked me anything about fruit or seed dispersal.

In an attempt to answer her, I said, "Well, Samantha that's a good observation, but Nature has provided the means for all these fruit trees to grow young ones. Samantha, do you and Andrew like fruits?"
She looked at me as if to say what a dumb question.
"Of course we do." She blurted out laughingly.
"You know we do papa," they both chuckled together.

"Sammy, most people love fruits and most animals do too. Birds, bats, and insects love to eat fruits. But do you think that they are as careful as you and Andrew to put the seeds in the garbage when they are finished eating the fruits?"
She laughed out aloud. "No, I don't think so papa. Eh, Andrew?"
He nodded his head indicating that he agreed with her.

I continued, "You see, fruits, like apples, pears, peaches, and plums that grow on big farms are picked and sold everywhere. When they're eaten, sometimes, the core, which contains the seeds or pits are thrown away. Some of them do germinate if they fall on fertile soil. Also some animals and birds do feed on fruits and berries directly on the trees, or on those that have fallen below the trees. At times, the feeding animals or insects will take the fruits or berries with them and eat them somewhere else. They eat the flesh of the fruit and will often leave the rest behind. In the case of berries, birds will swallow the pits, and pass them out unharmed wherever they empty their bowels."
"Do you mean nothing happens to the pits in the bird's stomach, Papa?"
"Well, I guess not. It seems that no harm comes to them, because the seeds do germinate when they fall in good soil with sufficient moisture. Sometimes though, during a rainfall, seeds are washed away into streams and carried by the water down stream. After a flood, they can be washed on land, where they might germinate. Of course, people grow plants from seeds as well."

After this long explanation, Samantha and Andrew nodded their heads as though they fully understood the explanation. Although, I am sure that they did not fully grasp everything that was explained to them, they were quite satisfied with the answer, and they did not question me further about seeds.

Walking down a slope, all the while still holding hands, we finally reached the lakeshore. The beach was a concave expanse of white and brown sand. Without wasting any time, Samantha and Andrew removed their running shoes and having secured them on an exposed root stump, they walked over to a small mound of sand.

Then the ever-vigilant Samantha said to me, while pointing to an exposed root stump, "Papa, how come I can see this root, but we cannot see the roots from those plants."
She pointed to some tall evergreen pine trees, on the hill a little distance away.

I decided that I will teach her a simple lesson in soil erosion, and hopefully she would learn it without a complicated explanation. This would be a practical lesson. I asked her and Andrew to bring me two sticks of wood. I planted each stick in a separate mound of sand. I asked Samantha to fetch some water in her little pail. This she did. I then asked her to keep throwing water against one of the mounds of sand, in which one of the sticks was planted.

The sand around this stick loosened and washed away gradually every time she threw the water against it. The lower part of the stick became exposed, and it eventually fell down.
Pointing to the fallen tree with its exposed roots, I said, "This is similar to what happened to that root stump. The water from the lake lapped constantly against it, gradually removing particles of soil, while the rains also helped to loosen and wash away the soil around the lower part of the tree."
The other stick of wood, the one on which she did not pour any water, remained standing with its lower part still covered with sand.

I continued in an effort to further reinforce my explanation, "See Sammy and Andrew, every time the water from the lake lapped against that exposed tree root, or when it rained, the water removed particles of soil from it, a little bit at a time. After this had been done over a period of time, the roots would lose their grip on the soil, and the roots would be unable to support the weight of the plant. Then all that is required for the tree to fall is for a

strong breeze to blow against it or a heavy rainfall to wash away the remaining soil. That's how the tree fell, leaving only this exposed stump of root. The other trees away from the lake, the ones, you pointed out to me which the waves from the lake did not strike, still have their roots buried in the soil, just like the stick, which you planted but did not throw water against." Pointing to the stick, which was still embedded in sand, I said, "See, this lower part of the stick, where the roots of the plant would have been, is still covered with sand. There is no wasting away of the soil, no erosion."
They both nodded their heads. I had just taught them a simple lesson in soil erosion by water.

From the mound of sand, which they had previously discovered, they cupped handfuls of fine-grained sand and allowed the sand to slither through their fingers.
"Look papa, look," said Andrew showing me his hands where sparkling specks of dust had adhered to his moistened and sweaty palms, "Are these diamonds, papa?"
"No Andrew," Samantha snapped, "Eh, papa, these aren't real diamonds, are they papa?"
"No, indeed not, my dear. These aren't real diamonds."
"See what I told you Andrew! I told you so. But, papa what are they?"
She too showed me her hands. The sparkling specks which glistened in the brilliant sunshine and shone like gold covered her hands up to her shoulders.

I tried to avoid a thorough explanation of the geological structure and formation of the rocks from which they were derived, as this would have been too advanced for their little untrained minds. I was certain that the specks were originally part of the eroded rocks.
"Wash your hands in the lake and come. Let us see where the golden particles came from."
Samantha and Andrew ran to the water's edge. Samantha was the first to return.
"Papa, I'm first."
"Samantha cheated Papa."
"Never mind, Andrew. You're here that's all that matters."

I took them to a nearby outcrop of what looked like red shale. I handed each a tiny bit taken from the outcrop, which was moistened by the early morning showers.
"Now let's crumble it. Watch me."
I took a small bit in my right hand, and using my index finger and thumb, I applied sufficient pressure to it while rolling my fingers and thumb together. I rubbed it on the top of my hand.
"Papa look, your hand is shining."
They both did the same to their hands. In a short time their hands too were covered with sparkling dust-like particles.

They giggled with delight. Samantha and Andrew covered their hands up to their elbows with the red shale. They rubbed each other's hand. Tiny silvery specks clung on to their sweaty skin and sparkled like diamonds in the bright sunshine.
"Look, Papa, look at my hands, aren't they beautiful Papa?" said Samantha.
"And mine too, Papa. Look, Papa look."
I looked at both their hands with renewed interest. The crystal-clear particles glittered in the sunshine.
"Nature has provided us with such beautiful things even where we least expect them," I said, "We need only to look for them."

We then proceeded to build sand castles, Samantha, Andrew and I. Using a broken piece of wood for a spade, I dug the sand. With bare hands, they scooped up the sand and each built a separate castle. I closely watched my little darlings as each tried to rival the other. Like eager beavers, they worked methodically. They crudely shaped their mounds of sand into castles. As their castles grew higher and higher, they had much difficulty in trying to get the sand to stay atop their structures.

"Look, Papa, mine's bigger than Andrew's, eh Papa?"
"No mine's bigger, eh Papa?" said Andrew.
I had to be careful to diffuse this potential threat to little Andrew's ego, and not to show favoritism to either one. Samantha's was indeed much bigger than Andrew's.
"Sammy aren't you bigger and older than Andrew?"
"Yes, I'm his bigger sister."
"Is that so Andrew?"
"Yes, Papa," was the reply.
"Then, I suppose it's ok if her castle is bigger than yours Andrew. As you grow older and get bigger then you too will build bigger ones."
He nodded in the affirmative.

It is truly amazing how quickly children learn to accept a simple straight forward, but truthful explanation. Rivalry is common among siblings, and a natural behaviour pattern, especially when the age difference is small. At a tender age, minors become very possessive. The use of the word "mine" becomes a major part of their vocabulary. Here they are beginning to assert themselves. At times it is important to point out little differences.
"See, Samantha, he is younger than you, therefore, less may be expected of him."

Having exhausted this quiet activity, they turned to another activity. Armed with small plastic pails, Samantha and Andrew strolled to the water's edge. Samantha waded into the clear water cautiously. Andrew, always a step behind, hesitated before putting his right foot into the water.

Most little children are naturally tentative when confronted with a strange situation. It is important to let them explore it gently by themselves, when there is no danger to their personal safety. By always saying, "no" to the child, and by being overly protective, we leave him or her no room for growth, but actually inhibit their progress. The water felt warm to the touch having been heated by the noonday sun. This encouraged Andrew to put in his left foot, and soon he had both feet in the water.

Close to the water's edge, was a rather big rock. It created a tiny pool whenever the slow moving tide came in and the water rushed over it. As the tide receded, and this happened constantly at short intervals, the temporary pool emptied itself. It filled up again when the next wave rolled in.

Samantha, holding Andrew's hand selected this spot to fill her bucket. She would fill her little pail with water, carry it a short distance on shore and repeatedly empty it. Meanwhile, little Andrew was having much difficulty maintaining his balance, because of the uneven, rocking motion of the waves. He attempted to fill his little pail, but his unsteady legs caused by the rocking motion of the waves made him slip. He ended up with his rear end wet all over, and unable to fill his little pail.

"Samantha, would you please fill Andrew's pail?" I asked.
"Ok, Papa."
She took Andrew's bucket, but insisted on filling hers first. In fact, that was what she did. While holding on to her own pail, she still attempted to fill Andrew's pail using her other hand. The result was that his pail was never full. Time and again, she would make sure to fill her pail. She carried it and emptied it. Then on her return, still holding on to her own, she would try to fill Andrew's pail.

I suggested to Samantha that after filling her bucket, she should put it down, and fill Andrew's. She didn't cherish this idea, because she must always be the first to empty her pail.
Yet there was an opportunity to teach her to be charitable towards her brother, so I said, " Be a good girl and help out your little brother. He really needs your help."
This time she did what I suggested. She was going to be a useful, bigger sister.

Looking at the sky, I noticed that the sun had crossed the mid-day point. I observed that they were becoming a bit tired of this activity. An effective way of relieving boredom, especially among children is to change activities constantly, or as soon as boredom begins to set in. Therefore, I suggested that we go for a walk. Samantha and Andrew agreed heartily. However, they started off only after they had planted slender sticks on top of their sandcastles, as if to say, "this is my property, and no one should touch it."

“Look, Papa Look! Mine's taller than Andrew's." and Samantha began to laugh teasingly.
"No, Papa, mine..." his voice trailed off as though he realized that it was useless to compete, for her castle was indeed taller than his.
“Never mind Andrew, as you grow bigger, one day you too will be able to build a really big one.”
“Ok, papa.”

It was so comforting to see how quickly their little differences were resolved. Sometimes it required just one word, a simple explanation, a suggestion, or an encouragement. Children love to please, but they relish attention. Sometimes they would try your patience to see how much they can get away with, or how far they can go. It is vitally important for grown-ups to listen to them. In fact when Samantha and Andrew said the word, “Papa.” They expressed it with such warmth and sincere love that I was encouraged to listen to them!

Ascending a gentle, sloping hill, and still walking in single file we gingerly placed our feet on the ground to avoid prickly leaves, pine cone needles, or thorn-like thistles. The climb was agonizingly slow. Almost every step the children took, they pointed to something that caught their attention, and we had to stop to examine it. In fact, they found interest in everything that moved. I then challenged them to play an observation game. “The first one to identify something by name wins a point.” You can readily imagine the enthusiasm with which they approached this activity.
“Look, Papa, a bug," said Andrew.
"It's a lady bug, eh Papa?" insisted Samantha.
"Yes, Samantha, it’s a lady bug." I said with resignation. Thank God, it was!

"Look, Papa, there’s a rock, just like my pet rock, eh Papa?"
"No, Andrew, it's like mine, eh Papa?" Samantha said this emphatically.
“First we must collect it and then we shall compare it.” I said, “This way we will be able to tell whose pet rock it really resembles."
"Ok, Papa. Andrew keep this one in your pail.”

They never seem to tire, nor did they lose interest in pointing out insects, or little scurrying lizards. Sometimes all they said was, "Look, Papa, look isn't it pretty?"
To which I replied, "Yes, it is pretty," even if I didn't think so. If I ever made the mistake of ignoring their comments, or if I neglected to acknowledge their observation, they would repeat it until I did. Another very important lesson is to acknowledge children's remarks directed at you, and respond to them as quickly as possible.

Having identified several life forms, and having exhausted this now famous 'See and Name game,' we finally emerged from the woods. It was hot and very humid. The heat was oppressive, and the sun's scorching rays burnt our exposed skin. We therefore sought the shade and tried desperately to avoid open spaces, as we attempted to beat a hasty retreat to the hotel.

As we came close to the hotel, there were several other distractions along the way that held their interest. In the distance, to our left, but clearly visible, was a beautiful rolling stretch of landscaped green. It was a magnificent golf course. Today, however, no one played golf. I supposed the weather was far too humid, hot and uncomfortable for anyone to enjoy a game of golfing. We stood up for a moment to admire the golf course.
"Can we go over there?" asked Andrew.
Before I could venture an answer, Samantha blurted out, "No, I don't think we are allowed. Eh Papa?"
To avoid follow-up questions and another potential argument, I simply said, "See, there's no one there. It is far too hot for anyone to be outside, it's best that we try to get to our air-conditioned room."

On the opposite side were several paved tennis courts enclosed by a fence.
"They play tennis there, eh Papa?"
"Yes, Sammy."
"And can we play too?" inquired Andrew.
"Certainly," I replied
"Can we play today, Papa?"
There was no need for me to answer Andrew.
"No dodo head. Didn't Papa say it was too hot, can't you feel the heat?" said Samantha.
"Papa, Samantha called me a dodo head. I'm not a dodo head, eh Papa." Andrew responded with some irritation.

I had to go to little Andrew's defense, "Samantha, didn't I tell you that you shouldn't call your brother by such names?"
"Andrew, I'm sorry, I didn't mean it."
"Then you should never use it." I replied.
"Sorry, Papa, I wouldn't do it again."
"But Sammy, you promised me that before." I reminded her.
"But Papa, sometimes my mouth slips. Maybe I should zip it up," she said, as she ran her index finger and thumb across her mouth. They both had a good laugh, and all was forgiven.

The path that led to the hotel curved to the left of the tennis courts. On the bend in the path, there was an indentation, a hollow in the road surface. This sunken portion of road was transformed into a natural mini lake, as water from the morning showers had settled in it.
"Look, Papa look, birds bathing." Samantha and Andrew were thrilled and excited to see those feathered friends frolicking.
"A natural bird bath," I said.

We stood still and watched doves, finches, sparrows and some other common species dart in and out of the water. It was a way of cooling themselves from the intense heat. They were having a ball. They jumped in, dipped their heads under the water, emerged, shook their wings, and pruned their feathers. What a wonderful sight!

Here Nature's creatures were taking full advantage of her kindness and goodness.
"Papa that's really a bird bath, eh Papa?"
"Yes, Sammy a natural bird bath."
"It is really a big one, eh Papa?"
"Yes, Andrew. It's really big!"
"What is a natural bird bath Papa?"
I half anticipated this question from Samantha. Children's ability to question and their curiosity arousal are signs of intelligence. Children's young and impressionable age is the ideal time for teaching and instructing them.

"Things that are made by people are called artificial, or man-made, and this is the opposite of natural, which is God-made. Have you ever heard of Terry Fox, Samantha? He was that famous and courageous Canadian who lost one of his natural legs to cancer. He jogged across Canada with one natural and one artificial limb to raise funds to help find a cure for cancer. A natural thing is one that is made or produced by nature. His artificial limb was man-made especially for him, to help him move about."

"So Papa, you mean that the bird bath formed by itself?
"Well, yes. I am sure no one deliberately dug the road to build this hollow so water would settle in it just for the birds to bathe in. Sometimes the earth moves up or down. Softer soil will tend to sink under heavy weight. When we get near the lake we will try this out.

The intensity of the sun's heat wave caused our enjoyment of this sight to be short-lived. Samantha, Andrew and I continued walking, but as we approached the temporary birdbath, the birds took to flight one by one, only to disappear among the pine trees. We followed the winding road, but walked under the shady pines to protect us from the hot, stinging rays of the sun.
"Why are we walking in the shade?" inquired Andrew.
"So the sun won't burn us, eh Papa?"
There was no need for any further explanation. I could always rely on Samantha to come up with a reasonable answer, and she has never disappointed me.

Hot and sweaty, we climbed a few low steps that led to the lobby of the Pine Isle Hotel. My intention was to check into our room for a cool drink and rest a while. Little did we realize, Samantha, Andrew and I, that the maid hadn't yet cleaned our room. She had just entered it. We decided to wait this out in the lobby.

We were in the perfect spot to see the attendants, maids, and vacationers as they passed by.
Andrew greeted the individuals as each one came by "Hiii," he lingered on the last vowel.
The passerby often responded in like manner, or with a smile. This one time, a young man came by, but did not acknowledge Andrew's greeting. Andrew was disappointed and visibly upset.
"Papa, he didn't say hi. Why didn't he say hi, Papa?" he kept repeating.
Samantha tried to come to my rescue, "Andrew he is working."
"No, he isn't, Samantha. That other man is." Andrew was referring to a man who had a bunch of tools hanging from a broad belt he wore around his waist.
Andrew was right. He still couldn't understand why the former didn't say hi, and this bothered him.
"Why, Papa, why Papa?"
I had to offer an explanation. "Maybe he didn't hear you, Andrew. Perhaps he was in a real hurry, or maybe something upset him."
Andrew did not ask why again, but this did not deter him from saying 'hi' to any other person who went by.

The maid who was cleaning our room was taking a much longer time than we had anticipated.
"Could we go out for another walk Papa?" I really didn't care to, neither did I want to, because it was so very hot, but again they were becoming restless.
"Ok," I said, "but only for a short while."
"Goody, goody." they shouted with elation.
Children possess boundless energy, and never seem to tire like adults, especially the elderly ones like me.

Thus, without any hesitation, Samantha, Andrew and I went off to a nearby forested area. Near the entrance of this forest lay a huge log, about thirty feet long and eighteen inches in diameter. It looked like one of those tall electric lamp poles. We sat on this log for a short while, surveying the scene of pine, shrubs and scrub bushes. Suddenly, Samantha stood on the log and attempted a balancing act. She fell off. Andrew, not to be deterred went to imitate her, but very soon, he too was on the ground.

"Let me help you both," I offered.
I took Samantha first, and holding her by the hand, I walked along the side of the log while she walked gingerly on the log. Gradually I released my hold. I was amazed at her coordination. After a few attempts, she seemed to have perfected the art of balancing on a log. Andrew surprised me. He mastered it rather quickly. Soon they began walking the whole length of the log. However, when they tried to walk too quickly, they would topple over and fall to the ground, which thankfully was covered with a layer of soft leaves. I reminded them that when they are attempting to learn a new skill, it is best to proceed slowly at first until they have mastered it. They repeated this balancing act several times increasing their walking speed on the log as they became more proficient. We had many laughs, especially when one of them slipped on to the ground, when trying to run on the log.

Soon however, I heard the now familiar words, "Papa, I don't want to play this game anymore."
Andrew was only waiting to hear this from Samantha.

"Papa, can we play something else?" he said this while he was walking the length of the log.
To baby-sit youngsters, one has to be resourceful. A rich imagination is a necessity and it will work wonders for you, especially on a hike where there are no computer games, television, or video games.

On the ground, there were numerous pine cones. I decided to make good use of this natural resource. "Let's prepare an enclosure, where we can put up buildings." It is important to participate in their games as far as practicable, as this encourages them in the activity. We removed leaves, broken twigs and cleared an enclosure.
"What are we going to use for buildings, Papa?"
I was prepared for this question. I knew it was coming. "Oh, let's use the pine cones. Do you know why they are called pine cones?"
It was Andrew who said, "Because they remind us of ice-cream cones."
"Yes, they are shaped like ice-cream cones."

They scampered here and there collecting pine cones of various sizes. These kids never seem to tire. Each tried to rival the other in the number of pine cones they were collecting. Having gathered quite an assortment, they arranged them side by side to form a giant rectangle.

"What shape have you and Samantha designed Andrew?"
He did not know.
"Do you know Samantha?"
"Of course!" she shouted.
"Well, what is it?"
"A square, Papa."
"Well, you are not quite right." I said.
She began to argue, "It is a square, Papa. I know."
"What is a square, Samantha?"
"It has four sides, Papa."
"That's correct, but there is something more to it."
"What Papa!"
"All the sides must be equal." I did not want to get into right angles, so I left it at that. "It is easy for us to find out whether it is a square or not. Let's measure the sides."
Using a straight piece of stick, we measured opposite sides. There were two long ones and two short ones.

“This is called a rectangle,” I said, “Remember a square has four equal sides, also in both the square and the rectangle all four-corners are shaped as a capital L.”
“So, we built a rectangle Papa?”
“Yes, dear, we did.”

They left an entrance and lined the sides of the rectangle with pine cones. Samantha then put three big cones to stand upright, each supporting the other.
"Here is where we live. This is our house, right, Andrew?"
For once, she sought her brother’s approval. He agreed.
"Andrew, hand me that small pine cone. That will be you," she said.

She had already placed a bigger one, which she called Samantha.
"Now this is daddy. This is mommy. This is you, Papa. This is Nana, and this is uncle Nick. Oh, I must not forget grandpa, Betty, Liz and uncle Mark and aunty Joyanne. Andrew, you go and get five more pine cones.”
She was really being bossy, and of course, Andrew began to offer some resistance. I had to remind her that it was a joint project.
“Sammy, you need to help him find more pine cones.”
She agreed and away they went in search of more cones.

They returned with extra pine cones.
"What should we feed them?" I asked innocently.
"Oh I saw nuts on the ground. Did you see nuts, Andrew?"
He nodded. They went in search of nuts. They brought as many as they could find.
"Now they have food to last them for a long time."
"Yes, Samantha enough food to last them for a long time,” I said.
"Papa, do you think they'll need a drink?" asked Andrew.
"I guess they will be able to get a drink when it rains, Andrew."
"Papa what shall we do next?"
“Samantha, I'm sure that our room is ready. Let's return to the hotel."

"But Papa, we can’t leave our family like that, they will get wet when it rains and they will catch a cold, eh Papa?"
"I suppose so, Samantha.
“Andrew, let's cover them up so they won’t get wet."
Samantha and Andrew collected handfuls of straw. They covered the people with straw. Then Samantha, Andrew and I left our pine cone

family, and the results of our labour. Interestingly enough, they never looked back at their forsaken family. Children are smarter than we give them credit for. They know what make believe is.

Making our way towards the hotel by another route, we encountered a well-groomed three- foot high hedge of evergreen shrub. This hedge bordered the entire length of the walk up to the hotel. Suddenly, Samantha stopped and pointed to a gaping hole in the fence.
"Papa, Papa, do you think a bird is building its nest there?"
"Not likely Samantha, I don't think a bird would want to lay its eggs where they can be seen easily and be interferred with."
"But Papa, you remember when you showed Andrew and me a purple Finch's nest on a pine tree near your house. Papa that nest was low."
"Yes, Samantha, you're quite right. You asked me if I thought a bird was building its nest there. Well dear, my answer is, I didn't think so."
She smiled and said nothing more.

I guess a straight- forward answer would have sufficed, but I attempted to give much more than what was expected. This is obviously a common fault that many adults make. A simple, straightforward question deserves a simple and direct answer. The child is not interested in details, unless the response demands it.

My short response did not discourage them, for with child like exuberance both Andrew and Samantha continued to draw my attention to any irregularities they observed in the hedge, which they thought were potential birds' nests.

Immediately behind the hedge were several pine trees and some deciduous trees.
Pointing to one of the trees, Samantha excitedly exclaimed, "See Papa, see a woodpecker, right Papa!"
She directed her tiny finger to a redheaded woodpecker, which was tap, tapping on a slender pine.
"I can't see it," said Andrew.

"Andrew you're blind. Look here," and she pointed her little hand in the direction of the bird.

"No, I can't see it Sammy."
"Andrew, look at where I'm pointing my finger."
"Yes Papa, I see it now."
"Maybe it is looking for insects to feed on," I said.
"No Papa, I don't think so Papa. It is building a nest. Woodpeckers build nests in tree trunks, right Papa?"
"Yes, Sammy."
"But he could be doing both."
Samantha nodded her head in agreement. I was surprised that she actually agreed with me.

What keen observation for a child of five I thought. It's truly amazing how children never seem to run out of things that interest them. Their curiosity is so easily aroused. They are resourceful, creative and rich in imagination. They see things as they are, literally. They do not like nor do they understand abstract solutions only concrete ones. Often they themselves will give some of the most logical answers, or come up with an unexpected solution.

Now standing in front of Pine Isle Hotel, Andrew pointed to some lights.
"Lights, eh Papa?"
Whereupon, Samantha chimed in, "Lots of lights so people can see the name, eh Papa?" she then proceeded to spell the name, letter by letter, "P-I-N-E I-S-L-E R-E-S-O-R-T."

Later that day, we dined at the Fishermen's Net, a seafood restaurant that boasts of having the widest assortment of seafoods. For dessert, Samantha was served a small bowlful of ice cream. Samantha began smudging her ice cream, playing with it by pushing it down with her spoon.
"Samantha, stop playing with your ice cream and eat it," said her dad. "What are you doing?"
"Oh, Daddy, I'm pushing in the ice cream so it will not fall off the bowl. Daddy, I think Andrew needs help with his ice cream."
By saying this, she diverted his attention from her. I smiled to myself in acknowledgement of her ploy that worked to perfection.

It was now late evening and it was time to return to the hotel. The air was still very dank and hot. We boarded the mini van on this sultry day with the van's air conditioning going full blast. Samantha and Andrew began to sing, "Row, Row, Row Your Boat." I supposed their boat must have sunk, because after singing "Merrily, merrily, merrily life is but a dream," all was silent. There was no more rowing and no more singing. They had fallen fast asleep. Great! Peace at last! Now I too can relax!

ROGER BRARRINGTON

Roger Brarrington was one of the strangest little creatures that one could find anywhere. He had long cascading ears, which almost touched the ground. His shiny coat was very furry dusty-yellow in colour. When baby Roger was born, his parents were sadly disappointed in the way he looked. "Isn't his colour unusually different for our baby?" said Pinky, his mother. "He certainly seems rather odd-looking to me," Cottontail, his father replied. "His body is covered with such very thick fur, very unlike his brother's and sister's!"

Roger was one of three babies born to Pinky and Cottontail Brarrington. Unlike the rest of the family, who had white fur coats and pink eyes that were small and round, Roger's eyes were neither pink nor small and round like the others. Indeed, they were very large, and charcoal black. His furry face tapered to a point and protruded outward like an ant-eater's head. "He certainly doesn't look anything like our other children," said his father, Cottontail. Pinky, his mother nodded her head in agreement.

Both parents, instead of being proud of Roger, showed their disappointment and displeasure in having him as one of their own. Even his brother Pouch and his sister Missy treated him differently. They often made fun of him. "The only thing we have in common with you, Roger, is your ability to hop like us." Roger did not know, nor did he think that he was any different

from his family, but it certainly did not take him long to realize it. This saddened him terribly.

Whenever the family took walks, or visited friends, everyone looked at Roger curiously. When his brother Pouch and sister Missy joined other young rabbits in play, they would not include him in their games, but often left him out because he did not look like any of them. Roger frequently heard such remarks as, "You 're not like us Roger, go away." "We don't need you to play with us today." "We can play without you." "Take a hike Roger!" In the face of such rejection especially by his very own brother and sister, Roger would feel sorry for himself. He would simply hop away sadly and hide behind any nearby bushes so he wouldn't be seen by anyone.

His own parents seemed ashamed of him, for when he accompanied them on their outings, they hid him in the background. They never introduced him as one of their own. So, Roger Brarrington grew to hate himself. He was often found wandering alone. Sometimes, he would stop near a pond and look sadly at his reflection in the clear water. Today he felt so very sorry for himself that he began to cry.

Mildred, the frog saw droplets of water falling into her pond. The droplets made ever widening circles as they hit the clear water in her pond. Mildred wondered how was this possible since the sky was so blue, and not a cloud to be seen anywhere. The sun was shining brilliantly, so there was no possibility of rain. The crystal clear water and the sun's rays allowed Roger to see himself quite clearly in the water. He looked closely at his reflection, but he couldn't figure out what was really wrong with him. As far as he was concerned, and in God's eyes, he was fine. He was a baby rabbit. That's all.

Mildred, the frog looked up and saw little Roger's large, black eyes now swollen and red from weeping and bathed in hot tears, that were streaming from his eyes. "Why are you crying, you poor dear?" asked Mildred. "Oh I don't know. I must be different. Just look at me, Mildred, just look at me. No one likes me. No one plays with me, and no one ever pays me any attention, not even my only brother and sister." "Well, I just did," said Mildred in a very kind manner. Roger continued, " Mildred, maybe I must be very ugly. I guess everyone thinks so, even my very own parents, for they never take me anywhere." He began to cry harder still.

"Come, come now you poor dear. Cheer up. It's certainly not the end of the world. Look at me now, Roger!" remarked Mildred in a soothing voice. "I'm certainly not pretty. I'm ugly and I know it. Everyone thinks so. Don't you think I'm ugly Roger?" "Not really Mildred, but in any case, you are like your kind. I am sure no one despises you," said Roger. "Really? That's what you think Roger, but I have news for you," replied Mildred. "Listen, only two days ago, some boys were throwing rocks at me. They were making strange faces at me. I am sure that they thought I was ugly. They teased me and hurled pebbles at me. Thank God I was able to dive under the water to escape their anger." Mildred added.

"But your eyes are beautiful!" said Roger. "I've heard it said that your eyes sparkle like diamonds, I believed Shakespeare was telling the truth, when, in one of his books he wrote that your eyes sparkle like diamonds." "You know who Shakespeare was, don't you Mildred? He was one of the greatest poets and playwright of all times. He wrote great stuff a long time ago." "Well if my eyes are as beautiful as Shakespeare said, how come no one has told me so, Roger?" "I just did." replied Roger. "Well Roger, I am sure that God has gifted you with something special." " If that's the case," responded Roger, "I don't think my family would agree with you." He hopped away sadly.

Roger moved on to rejoin his family. He searched everywhere, but he could not find them. He looked in his family burrow, but they were not there. His family had abandoned him, he thought to himself. Now he knew for certain that his family really did not care for him at all, for they were nowhere to be seen, not even one of them. "It really doesn't matter anyway," he sighed. "I guess, I am better off alone, and maybe it's better this way after all." He said to himself, then he shrugged his tiny shoulders and hopped sadly away. Now neglected, abandoned and forgotten by his family, Roger had to care for himself. He felt lost and lonely, but found himself a neat, little burrow hidden under a clump of trees. Though he was scared, he felt safe and secure in his new home.

Early each morning, before the sun rose, Roger went in search of food. He tried to avoid being seen by anyone. He felt self-conscious, awkward and quite useless. He never frolicked like the other animals. He lived a sad and lonely life. The sounds of crickets and the mournful hooting of the owls lulled him to sleep. There was no one to turn to when he was in need of help, no one to warn him of oncoming danger, and no one to comfort him.

Cool spring had given way to summer. The long summer days were pleasant and warm. The forest was alive with animals of every kind. He could hear birds singing merrily in the trees overhead, wild deer scampering madly everywhere, owls hooting, frogs bursting their lungs with their mating calls, doves cooing, squirrels chattering and badgers splashing in the clear water. However, it was the baying of the wolves that gave Roger a real scare. At such times, he would curl up into a very small ball in his burrow, while his little heart pounded feverishly with fear. There he would remain as quiet as a mouse.

Though summer had lingered beyond the usual three months, it too was now gone, and in its wake came fall. It saddened him to see all those golden, brown, yellow and red leaves fall to the ground. He was thankful for the evergreen pine and spruce trees that provided him with protection from his worst enemies, hunters and their hunting dogs. Fall had arrived damp and wet. He felt the chill in the air. He knew that it too would soon be gone, and the cold of winter would be here shortly, so he braced himself for its coming.

Roger though, was thankful for his one great blessing, his very thick, furry coat. It afforded him adequate protection from the coldness through the long and dreary winter months. This year, winter was particularly very cold, damp and bleak. He dearly missed his family. “I would rather take their insults than this loneliness,” he mused. It would have pleased him greatly to have just one glimpse of them; unfortunately, he never saw them again.

It was now the middle of December and Christmas was in the air. All the animals were having fun celebrating the Christmas season with parties. Some animals were attending parties at their friends’ homes, while others were hosting parties for themselves, and their friends. It really did not matter who was having a party. Every one without exception was welcome to attend. Somehow, Roger became caught up in the Christmas spirit. For once, he stopped feeling sorry for himself. “I shall go out and have some fun,” he said to himself. “I can’t gain anything by staying hidden all the time.” he reasoned.

On this day, the morning was invitingly bright and sunny. The air was crisp, refreshing and invigorating. Frosty branches glistened in the brilliant sunshine. Roger had never felt better. He hopped sprightly out of his burrow. He stretched his limbs, wriggled his ears, and sniffed the cool air. Then, after shaking the dust off his coat vigorously, he took off briskly to join in the celebrations.

In the trees high above, Roger heard laughter and merrymaking. The birds were having their annual Christmas party. There were music, dancing, singing, chattering and pleasant noises. "Hey there, Ozzi, can I join your party?" said Roger to an owl in the tree above. "Oh, certainly!" said Mr. Owl heartily. "Come on up Roger. Come on up. We’ll be only too happy to have you!”

In his excitement, Roger jumped up as high as he could go. He got on one low branch and could not climb any farther. He just stood there clinging to the branch. "What are you waiting on Roger?" shouted Twinky, the red finch. "Oh, I can't reach you,” said Roger disappointedly. “I don’t have wings and I can't fly." "Never mind," said Shirley, the kind-hearted robin. "We will lend you some feathers. Get back on the ground, and we'll meet you there." Roger used his limbs and lowered himself to the ground.

All the birds fluttered down and joined Roger on the ground. Each one gave him a feather. The birds painstakingly glued the feathers on to

Roger's body. He looked beautiful in his multicolored tunic. All the birds cheered and marvelled at Roger's new image. Roger, now bedecked with feathers, actually felt great as he had never felt before. "Wow you look beautiful Roger! Now you can join us Roger," they shouted gleefully. Each one flew back to the large spreading tree to await Roger's arrival and to resume their frolicking and merrymaking.

Roger, now feeling as proud as a peacock, stretched out his artificial wings. He leapt and made several attempts to fly but each time he landed back on the ground. "Keep trying Roger," they shouted with encouragement; but poor Roger became increasingly frustrated with every attempt, and cried out in frustration, "What's the use? What a waste of time! I always knew that I am useless." He thanked them, ripped off the feathers; and hopped away a lonely, dejected and disconsolate figure.

As he hopped along, Roger again heard much laughter and merrymaking. The haunting sounds of music attracted his attention, and he went to investigate. The sounds of music took him near a small clear stream. The badgers were having a Christmas party. All the animals that lived in water, or had their homes near water were invited guests. "Hey there, Bart, old pal," said Roger, "Can I join you folks?" "Certainly Roger, everyone is welcome. Just Jump in," said Bart, the badger. "Thanks much," replied Roger; and he became excited, especially when he saw his friend Mildred, the frog. Then Roger remembered that he could not swim. "Hey Bart, Mildred, I can't join you 'cause I can't swim," said Roger. "Just get on a log, you'll be safe and you can join us." They said.

Roger thought that was a brilliant idea, so he climbed on to a floating log. He tried to walk but he was used to hopping. He felt much more comfortable hopping. As Roger made the first hop, the log rolled in the water and down went Roger. He was a very poor swimmer. His thick furry coat got wet and became heavy with water. Worst still, the water was freezing cold. Roger managed to jump out off the water, and he shook the water off his coat. He eyed the log, but made no further attempts to climb on the log again. He knew the same fate would await him, and that he would end up in the water once more. Therefore, he gave up the idea, saying to himself, "I knew it. It's no use. I'm a failure. I am useless. See, I can't walk. I can't climb. I can't fly and I can't even swim. I'm useless." "I am a failure. I knew it all along. Why was I born anyway? I'm going home." Roger said this aloud. He was sad and so disappointed in himself that he hated everything. He wanted nothing to do with anyone, and he wished to be alone away from any other living animal. "Why, oh why was I born this way?" He was confused as he shook his head in utter dismay.

Lonely and dejected, Roger Brarrington hopped slowly away in a state of confusion. Being in this sorry state, he did not notice that he had wandered far away from his den. Worse yet, he wasn't aware that the weather had changed drastically. Wild and furious blasts of cold winter winds began to gust fiercely. The snow squalls quickly became blinding. Snow began to drift everywhere. Roger was forced to try to return to his home to seek shelter from the elements. He stumbled repeatedly in the freshly fallen snow; but his instincts kept him moving in the direction of his burrow.

"Soon, I would be home." He thought to himself, as he struggled blindly in the heavy snowfall. Then, close by, he heard feeble, squeaking noises. It sounded like a call for help. It came from behind a clump of trees. Millie, a baby mouse was lost. She was crying her little heart out. Roger hopped that way and saw baby Millie shivering in the cold. Her little gray coat was wet and she was half-buried in the snow. Her little tail was frozen. Her teeth chattered uncontrollably from the coldness. Roger felt such deep sorrow for this helpless little creature, that he was moved to tears. "What are you doing out in the cold, little baby mouse? Why are you here all alone in this weather?"

"Oh, I--I--I don't know where they 're. I've lost my dad and mom. We were just returning from a Christmas party, then the snow came, and I became separated from them," said Millie sobbing all the while. There was no way Roger would be able to find Millie's parents. The snowdrifts were too high. In less than an hour, Millie would be dead. He thought about taking her to his burrow, but this was an impossible task. In any event, she would not be able to withstand the cold any longer. "Never mind little one, I'll take care of you tonight. In the morning, I'll help you find your parents." Millie was too weak to speak. She simply nodded her head in grateful thanks.

Roger dug himself a hole in the snow. He covered baby Millie with his thick, furry body. Baby Millie felt snug and warm. They were both tired, so they soon fell fast asleep. All night long, the winds howled among the trees. It became bitterly cold as the wind chill factor plunged the temperature to well below freezing.

At long last morning came. The bright sunshine glistened like diamonds on the icy crystals hanging from the branches of trees. It was beautiful to witness Nature's changed scene. Armfuls of snow were cushioned snugly in the forked branches of trees, and mounds of white fluffy snow formed little hills wherever the snow had drifted.

Millie's parents, Georgie and Lorie kept an all night vigil in the hollow of a tree trunk. They did not sleep a wink all night, as they feared the worst for poor little Millie. They were certain that Millie was dead. No one could have survived this onslaught of cold weather without adequate cover. They hoped they would find her tiny body and give her a decent burial.

They searched everywhere. Then they stumbled on this snow-covered ball of fur, which looked like a tiny mound. Peering from under this frozen ball of fur were two beady eyes. They were Millie's. "Oh, Millie, Millie, you poor little dear," said Lorie, " You're alive! Your father and I were so worried that we stayed awake all night long. We were sure you didn't make it." "Thank Roger," said Millie. "He was the one who saved my life. When he found me, I was almost frozen to death. He risked his life to save mine. He sheltered me under his thick heavy fur coat. Isn't he wonderful, brave and beautiful!" said Millie. "Indeed he is! He certainly is!" replied Georgie and Lorie.

"Mom, dad, we must reward Roger. We must take him home to spend Christmas with us," said Millie, "Roger, Roger, wake up! It's morning. Thank you for saving our dear little girl's life," added Georgie. There was no answer. They started working on Roger immediately to wake him up. They scratched the snow off his thick, furry coat, jumped on his back, pulled on his ears, and blew hot air on his body. They allowed the sun's rays to thaw him out, and to warm his body. After some time, Roger's slender long ears twitched slightly. Then after a few more seconds had passed with the pleading voices of Georgie, Lorie and Millie ringing in his ears, Roger slowly stretched out his limbs one by one. Finally, he righted himself on his legs and took a couple of small hops, staggered, and looked around. Then he saw Millie and her parents. He smiled at them, and got up to leave.

"Thank God, Roger, you're alive!" shouted Georgie. "Roger, you risked your life to save our dear little Millie. Thank God that you had such very thick fur to keep our baby Millie warm! You are the greatest Roger! You are our hero. Now come with us, Roger, you must celebrate Christmas with us. We have lots to eat and drink." Just this once in his life, Roger felt really good about himself. He was very pleased that he had made such great use of the one precious gift that God in His bounty had given him, his thick furry coat. With it, he was able to save Millie's life. "After all, I am really useful." "Thank You God," he said humbly, as he smiled

contentedly to himself. He thought to himself, 'Mildred, the frog was right.' God has blessed each one of us with special gifts, but it is important for us to know what these gifts are and try to develop each to the best of our abilities, for the benefit or the betterment of others."

Roger accompanied Millie, Georgie and Lorie to their home. It was so refreshing to feel like somebody again, and to be appreciated for doing something good. Roger Brarrington, the rabbit was treated to the best meal he ever had, and he enjoyed the best Christmas ever. From then on, Roger never felt sorry for himself again. He continued to make the best of the gifts that God gave him, and tried not to pretend to be somebody or something that he was not. After all, his rich, thick fur had saved his life too.

Minty, Marty and Mildred

Randy, a quiet old man, whose wife had recently died, lived alone in a comfortable apartment in downtown Hamilton, a city of about 350,000 in South Eastern Ontario. Since his dear wife's sudden death, he kept two beautiful pet cats as companions. He named them Minty and Mildred.

Minty and Mildred were both beautiful domestic short hair cats. Mildred, the older of the two, had a mixture of white, yellow, brown and gray coloring. Minty was a mixture of white, yellow, gray and black. They both had green eyes and long fluffy tails.

Randy never intended to rear more than two pets. However, on a visit to a Pet store one day to purchase some cat food, he saw this very cute, white pet rat. Its unusually lovely pink eyes and furry coat attracted him. Randy took an instant liking to this handsome little fellow. He promptly bought this little, fluffy rat, took him home and named him Marty.

He introduced Marty to Minty and Mildred, and told them that they should always be kind to Marty, and treat him as their little brother. From the outset, Mildred took an instant dislike to Marty. She showed her displeasure by exposing her teeth as she hissed at him. She did this whenever she passed his cage. Moreover, she would reach out with her front paws and slap Marty's cage, trying to intimidate him. Whenever Randy was around, she would pretend that she was playing fondly with Marty. If she happened to rest near Marty's cage, he would hide in the farthest corner of his cage away from her; for fear that she would harm him.

Minty was not as unwelcoming as Mildred. Neither did she seem to possess Mildred's jealous streak. At first, Minty was not too pleased to have Marty around, but she soon came to accept him as one of the family and she never displayed any anger or hostility towards Marty. Actually, she developed a soft spot for the little fellow, as he was always so kind, affectionate and willing to please.

Randy was very particular with the way he raised his pets. Minty and Mildred each had separate bowls from which they ate. They lapped up milk or water from their own liquid containers. Each cat had her own spacious cage in which she napped during the day, and slept during the night. On special occasions, or if thunder roared heavily at night, during inclement weather, he invited them into his bedroom, where they curled themselves up and slept at the foot of his bed.

Randy always wanted the best for his pets. Whenever and wherever Pet shows were being held, Randy made it his business to be present. Once there, he would inquire from the organizers about eating habits of cats, and the quality of food that best met their needs. He was particularly interested in the prize- winners and would speak to the owners to see what he could learn from them.

He discovered that not too many of them were willing to share the secrets of their animals' successes. Some cat owners tried to encourage him to enter his pets in competitions, but others were reluctant to do so. He often thought about entering his cats, but he was determined to ensure that if his cats did not win prizes, at least they should make a good showing and rate highly in the eyes of the judges and the onlookers.

Randy was a thoughtful and considerate man with a scientific mind. Pet store-owners suggested to him food brands that sold very well. He tried feeding them to his pets, but he did not see any significant changes in the condition of his cats. The owners of prize winning cats really did not like to share their secret recipes with him. Some told him what they fed their cats, but Randy did not always believe them. He decided that he would find out for himself, which brand of cat food had the best effects on cats' general health, including their appearance, hair growth, gloss and disposition.

Randy read and studied many advertisements. He made numerous inquiries. He studied the labels on the packages and read the information about their contents carefully. Being the conscientious pet owner that he was, Randy felt that he would not be satisfied until he tested each product by feeding it to his cats. He understood that many good companies did quality research, but there were some that made exaggerated claims. He certainly intended to verify the respective claims himself.

Randy had read and had also heard a lot about the effectiveness of the MAIS Cat Food. He planned to test this product to see whether it had the desired effect in producing successful healthy animals. This experiment would last for about three months, which would give him sufficient time to note the products' effectiveness, and to see whether it really worked as the manufacturer had claimed it would.

Randy decided to feed the MAIS product to Minty. She was more likely to accept it, as she was not as fussy, nor as temperamental as Mildred. He was quite certain that if it proved successful, Mildred too would readily take to it. Meanwhile, he would continue to feed Mildred the usual stuff that he always fed them. He also offered small quantities of MAIS to Marty, the little white rat. Marty enjoyed it, and often wanted more.

Several months later, Randy could not help observing the differences in his pets. Minty became even more lady-like. She was so calm and contented. She had a wonderful disposition. Her coat became glossy and thick like a new plush rug. Her fur coloring was rich. She was in the pink of health. Even Marty grew noticeably healthier. His white coat glittered in the light.

Though Randy had noticed the obvious difference, he wanted to see if other people shared his findings. He observed that Mildred had become even more short tempered. He did not understand why, but he dismissed it as one of her usual traits. In any event, he planned to start her on the MAIS product if his observations were found to be correct. First, he would see what others had to say, and whether they would confirm his findings.

Randy did not have to wait very long. On a sunny Saturday afternoon at Eastgate Square in Hamilton, the National Cat Show competition was scheduled to be held. It attracted all breeds of cats and cat lovers. There were Red Tabbies, Smoke Persians, Calicoes, Manx, Silver Tabbies, Abyssinians, Burmese, White Longhair, Domestic Shorthair, and some other mixed breeds.

Randy entered both Mildred and Minty. Each shared a separate cage. Randy stood proudly beside his pets. However, he noticed the great deal of attention that was being given to Minty. He overheard such remarks as, "What a beauty!" "What splendid colour! Look at her glossy coat!" "What a specimen!" "She looks so healthy, and she has such great physical conditioning!" Randy was beside himself with joy. He was elated.

Mildred was given some curious glances, but no one paid her any special attention. She felt angry, and was obviously jealous. She noticed the amount of attention that Minty had received. Minty stood tall exuding confidence, as though she knew that she was a winner. At the end of the competition, and to no one's surprise Minty was declared the best overall winner. Minty's cage was bedecked with the winner's blue ribbon. Randy was very happy for Minty. He took home a huge trophy. However, Mildred, instead of congratulating Minty, became insanely jealous of her.

Mildred knew that she was not being fed the same MAIS cat food as Minty and Marty, because after feeding them the MAIS cat food, Randy would stack it away and deliberately feed her the usual old brand. She never understood why he did that, but assumed that he preferred Minty to her. Indeed she had a secret longing for the MAIS food, but had never been given even a taste. Now more than ever, she was convinced that Randy did not really care much for her, and it was the MAIS product that caused Minty to win first prize. This thought got her even more enraged, and secretly she began to despise them all.

Now that Randy had seen the results of the MAIS product, he was sold on it. He intended to start Mildred on it, first thing in the morning when he returned home. He believed that the next time it would be Mildred's turn to capture the top prize, or at the very least to share the honour with Minty. Randy had never communicated his intention to Mildred, so obviously she did not know nor did she understand what his plans were

On his way home from the show, Randy stopped at a pet store and bought a new, big bag of MAIS cat food. He was very fond of his animals; therefore, he was prepared to do anything to make their lives happier. However, all the way home, Mildred sulked. She felt bitter, hurt and disappointed. Whenever she recalled the applause, the congratulations and the attention that were showered on Minty, she became insanely jealous. Not knowing what Randy was planning for her, she secretly thought out a plan as to how she could secure all the MAIS cat food for herself.

On reaching home, Randy strolled proudly to Marty's cage. "Marty, old chap, I have such good news for you." "Look at this beautiful trophy and this Blue ribbon that Minty won. Our very dear Minty won not only in her category, but she also captured the best overall prize!"

For Mildred, hearing this was the final straw. She was livid. She sulked, withdrew and hid herself. Randy knew she was disappointed. However, he also knew that he would make it up to her starting with the MAIS food formula, first thing in the morning. Randy decided that he would feed her generous amounts of the MAIS cat food product. Of course Mildred was not told a word about Randy's plans for her.

As a result, moody Mildred had other plans of her own. "Never again would I suffer such humiliation," she said to herself. "But first, I need to get rid of Marty, Minty and Randy, then I will have everything to myself, especially all that MAIS food." Mildred was too hurt to think clearly. She allowed her jealousy to control her thoughts, and she decided to lash out blindly. It did not matter who got hurt.

She felt that tonight was the perfect night to make her move. It was Saturday. Randy usually got his weekend newspaper around 7pm. Randy had trained Mildred to bring in his daily newspaper. He usually left his front door slightly ajar so Mildred could drag his papers inside, and he could see the paperboy when he made his rounds collecting.

Tenants had complained to the Superintendent of the building about a mouse that was causing a great deal of damage to their property. In an effort to get rid of this nuisance, the superintendent had placed a set mousetrap two doors away from Randy's apartment in the corridor. Randy had warned Mildred and Minty many times of this potential danger. Tonight, however, Mildred decided that she would make good use of this trap. She would put it under Randy's bed, and this would take care of Marty. She was sure that Marty would fall for the cheese in the trap.

Mildred knew that whenever she took the papers to Randy, he usually buried his head behind them and raised it only when the newspaper carrier knocked on the door to indicate that he was collecting his money. Mildred felt that this would give her the opportunity, and sufficient time to drag the trap quietly and place it under Marty's bed.

As for Minty, Mildred intended to lock her up in her cage from the outside. This would prevent her from escaping. Once there she could starve to death. Randy was the problem, but she thought she had it all figured out. On Saturdays, Randy always went to bed immediately after the eleven o'clock news. He generally fell asleep instantly and always slept with the covers over his face. She would tie the ends of the covers to the bed- posts so he would not be able to escape.

Mildred worked herself into a frenzy, as she thought her plans through and speaking to herself said: "Randy deserves what's coming to him. I hate them all. He cheated me and he had no right to do that! As for Minty and Marty, I would rather live without them. They think that they are so cute and special. I'll teach them, I'll teach them!" She ran these thoughts through her head again and again. During this time, she thought only of the MAIS Cat food and what it would do for her. "Now I will have it all to myself, and I will be the prettiest and healthiest cat in all the world," she selfishly thought.

It was Saturday night and Mildred began to put her plan into action. She dutifully dragged in the daily newspaper and rested it at the Randy's feet. He diligently picked it up and began reading it. She slipped out again noiselessly, and quietly dragged the mousetrap and placed it under Randy's bed, then curled herself into a ball in her cage and pretended to be fast sleep.

As midnight approached and Randy slept peacefully. Mildred got up and locked Minty in her cage. She then opened Marty's cage, and enticed him to come out and play. He was reluctant to do so, especially as he knew that Mildred was not especially fond of him, but he couldn't resist the open door. He felt it would be nice to get out for a little exercise.

Silently Mildred stalked into Randy's bedroom. He was fast asleep. Her plan was working to perfection she thought. All was still. She set to work. She tied the far ends of the covers to the foot of the bedposts. Then she moved to the top of the bed near Randy's head.

Marty meanwhile had scurried out of his cage to enjoy his new- found freedom. He was happy to join Mildred in play if he could only find her. He did not realize that a trap was set under Randy's bed to catch him. He ran around Minty's cage. His noise awakened Minty. She peered into Mildred's cage. Mildred was nowhere to be seen. This was unusual, for Mildred always slept in her cage. Minty stretched her legs and tried to get out of her cage. The cage was locked. This too, was strange. It was always left open. She suspected that Mildred was up to something.

Minty had noticed Mildred's strange behaviour earlier during the day. She was accustomed to Mildred's mood swings, and she did not think much of it then. Now, however this was different. "Randy never let Marty out of his cage." "Why would he do it tonight?" Minty wondered about this. "Would Mildred harm Marty? ...And where was she? I am a prisoner in my own cage." These thoughts flooded Minty's head.

Meanwhile, Mildred jumped nimbly on Randy's bed. He was sleeping soundly. She positioned herself over Randy's face to reach one of the top corners of the bed sheet. Randy was dreaming that he had difficulty breathing. That he became dizzy and felt faint. Mildred pressed her body against his face as she gripped the end of the cover sheet. In a few seconds more Randy would possibly be stifled to death, she thought with satisfaction.

In the meantime, Marty was frisking around Minty's cage. She said to him, "Marty, please unlock my cage." Marty wasted no time. He used his sharp little teeth and tiny claws and released the small bolt. They both headed straight for Randy's bedroom. Minty saw nothing unusual. All was quiet. Randy appeared to be sound asleep.

Marty though was attracted by the smell of cheese. He darted under the bed and headed straight for the trap. With her keen eyes, Minty saw the trap. She knew at once why it was there. Suddenly she sprang at Marty to cut him off from the baited trap. Marty spun around instantly. As he did so, his long tail sideswiped the bait, and sprang the trap. The steel wire made a loud noise as it made contact with the wooden base. This sudden impact jolted Randy from sleep. In a daze, Randy's hands involuntarily flew to his face. Mildred was unable to disentangle her grip. Randy felt a soft furry body. He held on fast to it.

Still in a daze from being suddenly aroused from sleep, he clutched Mildred in his grasp, and tightened his hold. Mildred growled, hissed and screamed. She lashed out with her paws, scratching and clawing. Randy held on. Then opening his eyes, he saw Mildred. She scowled and glared at Randy. He looked at her wonderingly. "Mildred, what's the matter? Why are you so mad?" He loosened his grip on her.

Suddenly Mildred jumped out of his hands bolted, and made a mad dash for the MAIS Cat food. She tore the bag with her claws and started eating ravenously. Randy followed her into the kitchen. Instantly, on seeing what Mildred was doing, Randy understood the cause of her strange and bizarre behaviour. "Mildred, don't you know how much I care for you?" Said Randy. "I bought these bags of MAIS Cat food, so I can start you on it in the morning. I am tempted to punish you and put you away for good Mildred. You are acting as though you are crazy with jealousy." Randy thought for a while then added, "I suppose you did not understand what I had intended to do. I must also blame myself. I failed you by not explaining the plans I had for you. I should have known better. Communicating with others is such an important factor in everyone's life."

In the morning Randy took Mildred to the veterinarian, so she could be treated for distemper. Randy also took along with him the MAIS food product. He asked the veterinarian to feed her with generous amounts of the food. This she did, and Mildred loved her for it.

After several weeks of treatment, Mildred was pronounced well. She had missed her family and now was ready to return home. She rejoined Randy, Minty and Marty, and together they were a happy family. Straight away, she went to Randy snuggled up to him, and licked his face. Then she went to Minty and rubbed noses with her.

They frisked together naturally. She strolled up to Marty's cage, lowered her head and purred affectionately. Two weeks later, she was entered in a feline contest and won handsomely. Both Randy and Minty cheered for her and when she came home with her first place blue ribbon prize and showed it to Marty, together they sang, "Happy Days are here again!"

TIMBU

In the wilderness of Africa lived Timbu, the baby elephant. From birth, Timbu was rather frail and weak. His skinny legs wobbled when he walked and he had great difficulty keeping up with the herd of elephants, to which he belonged, and which roamed the vast, grassy plains of Uganda. Ever so often, his older, stronger sisters and brothers would nudge him with their tusks to get him to walk faster. Sometimes, they even pushed him aside out of their way, as they felt that he was holding them back. They often poked fun at him. "Timbu, you skinny bone, you're so weak and frail, it's no wonder that your tusk won't grow. You are a slow poke. Can't you even keep up with us? Must we always wait on you?"

Sometimes, his mother and father had little patience with him. They seemed not to care much about him. On the hunt, they would leave him trailing far behind. Occasionally, Simba, his only sister would turn to him and encourage him to move on. Although she was usually kind to him, she did not like to wait on him either.

In any event, little Timbu deliberately walked slowly, as he disliked the reckless manner in which his family approached the business of feeding themselves. For example, while feeding, all the elephants present, including his family would rip the leaves from the nearby trees, break their branches and strip off all the bark from the trees leaving them bare. They even uprooted tall trees to get at the young leaves. Timbu often became angry with them, and showed his displeasure by wandering off in another direction, because he hated the idea of destroying nature's beautiful trees.

When the elephants were through feeding, they usually left that part of the forest a tree-less waste land. Timbu would often say to them. "Are you satisfied? Look at what you have done to our trees. You have destroyed the source of our food. Our forest is dying, and you are killing it. Shame on you. Soon we won't have anywhere to live or hide. Don't you think about the future? Don't you think of your very own little dear children that will be born in the future?"

"Look who's talking!" His eldest brother, Kimbu added rather teasingly. "It's no wonder that you're so puny and weak. Would you rather starve yourself to death?"
"Of course!" added Santo, his other brother, in a sarcastic tone of voice, "Timbu," he continued, "you are a real Sad Sack, you do nothing but complain. Luckily, no one listens to you. Don't you think it's far better to destroy those trees than starve ourselves to death?"
"Well put Santo, well put." Said Kimbu.

Timbu, knowing that he was no match for his brother's wits, would lower his head and quietly walk away. He felt terribly hurt and upset that his family showed such little regard and concern for God's earthly creation. As they walk away, Timbu would watch them at a distance with sadness in his little eyes as he continued feeding on shrubs. At times, he would use his tiny trunk to spray the saplings with water.

One bright, warm, sunny day in July with scarcely a cloud in the sky, the herd of elephants to which Timbu belonged set out on their usual feeding expedition. They walked about a mile and devoured every plant in sight. Moreover, they crushed everything in their path. They made very loud noises as they trumpeted and trampled the ground. They attacked and destroyed every living plant in sight leaving none standing. As usual, Timbu trailed far behind.

In the bushes just ahead of him, he could distinctly hear strange noises. The sounds were those made by human voices. Whoever these strangers were, they were speaking excitedly. Then Timbu saw them. They looked like sightseeing tourists; for they were carrying not only binoculars, but riffles too! This puzzled him. “Why did they need guns?” He thought to himself. “Maybe they needed them for protection from the big, ferocious cats.”

Emerging from behind a huge mahogany tree, was a big sunburnt, red-faced man, with an ugly grin, somewhat like a scowl on his face. He spoke to another bearded man, whom he called Jim. "Hey Jim, see those beauties!" "Yea, Mack, what gorgeous ivory tusks!" "Yea, they're worth a fortune; I'm sure, except for that skinny little fellow trailing behind. He has such a puny tusk! Pity him. He's not worth wasting a shot on." "I agree with you." Said Mack.

Then it dawned on Timbu that these men must be hunters. The cruel men aimed their riffles at the unsuspecting herd. Bang! Bang! Bang! Several shots rang out in quick succession. Four big, healthy elephants lay dead on the ground. The others scampered to safety, leaving that horrid scene behind. They bulldozed their way into the forest and stampeded every animal that happened to be in their path.

Poor Timbu had just witnessed the wanton slaughter of some of his family members, and he fled to safety as fast as his tiny legs would carry him. His little heart pounded feverishly. He trembled uncontrollably and felt nervous and weak. His unsteady legs very nearly buckled under his weight as he fled the scene. In the distance, he thought he saw his mother and father running; but he wasn't quite sure. He was certain of one thing: -his brothers didn't escape, because they all lay dead on the ground, killed by the riffles of those vicious and hideous hunters.

In the past, Timbu usually felt sad, and often got angry when he saw his family destroying Nature. However, he knew that they did this to survive. They needed food. To be killed unsuspectingly by human beings in ones' own native land saddened and grieved him more. It hurt so much that he felt sick to his stomach. He knew now that he and his family were no longer safe, not even in their homeland.

"Aren't human beings supposed to be kind, thoughtful and caring, especially to dumb animals?" he mused. "Then why, why should they want to kill us?" Timbu was truly baffled. He was still trembling from the shock of the wanton killing he had just witnessed. He lowered his head, and bending his tired legs, sank to the ground to rest.

Rest did not come easy however! No matter how hard he tried, Timbu just couldn't rest peacefully. In fact, he kept hearing loud noises. Turning his head in the direction of the sounds, he saw some men hacking at the ivory tusks of his dead siblings. They bagged the tusks and left the remains, elephant carcasses-on the ground. “What a waste! What a waste!” Timbu thought sadly, “and my brothers at that!” He felt faint.

Timbu took a long and heart-wrenching look at his brothers' corpses. He felt numb with grief and began to wander aimlessly as if in a daze. Instinctively though he moved cautiously, almost silently among the bushes trying to hide himself where ever he could. He trudged along for what seemed an eternity. Suddenly he heard some boisterous laughter, which seemed to come from what looked like a crude little hut.

He drew just close enough to the hut to hear what they were saying. The hunters were drinking and boasting. "AL, did you see that shot! Boy, I got him squarely right between the eyes!" said Mat.

"Yeah, and I scored a bull's-eye." added Pete. "He rolled over like a giant log." "Well, he's an elephant, what did you expect Pete? Do you suppose that he would roll over like a bit of candy cane?" said Jim to a roar of laughter.

Timbu couldn't take it any longer. He had heard enough. He felt really ill. His brothers were slaughtered and these evil men were joking about it. He must get away as far as possible from these cruel and hard-hearted men. These were men who killed for greed and made fun of it. He wondered what had become of his sister, Simba. Was she still alive? She was the only one who sometimes thought kindly of him.

Tired and feeling depressed, Timbu drifted off to the nearby river to get himself a drink of water. What he saw next paralyzed him. He saw three men wearing hardtop hats and khaki trousers. They had revolvers strapped around their waists. They were resting under some trees and talking in a low tone of voice, almost in whispers. Timbu froze. He tried to hide behind a tree by making himself really small, but they saw him!

"Are they going to shoot me too? Would they spare my life? My little ivory tusk is so tiny. Then again look at what those other men did." These thoughts ran through Timbu's mind. The men approached Timbu in a deliberate, business-like manner. Timbu made no attempt to run. He knew it was useless to try and outrun bullets that hit its target with lightening speed. Timbu was prepared to die. Quietly he whispered. "Great Spirit, be kind to me. I never destroyed your trees. I tried not to be mean to anyone. Please, Great Spirit, help me."

The men walked slowly towards him. They came closer and closer. Timbu lowered his head expecting the worst. He closed his eyes. Then he felt a tender hand run across his bony back. It rested on his head. Next, he heard a rather gentle voice. It was Tom's, the team's leader. "Poor little fellow, don't be frightened. We won't hurt you. You have already been through enough."

The other two men, Jack and Bill, patted Timbu's back and stroked his flanks softly. Tom continued, "Well little one, we are after some evil men. We call them poachers. They destroy animals wantonly and take away only certain parts of the animal that will fetch them a great price. They are full of greed. Maybe, you can help us by leading the way to these men." Timbu rolled his eyes as though he understood what was said to him. He gazed at them timidly. "Lead the way little fellow, we'll follow you."

Timbu raised his head and lowered it a few times to show that he had understood what was said to him. He moved slowly and led the way. He chose a path that took them close to where the dead elephants lay. Tom, Jack and Bill, who were game wardens, shook their heads several times in disgust. They felt very sad indeed as they looked at the discarded carcasses.

It is an accepted fact that elephants possess good memories. Timbu remembered where he had seen the hut. He walked towards it with the game wardens following closely. He made as little noise as possible. When they were close to the hut, the game wardens took cover behind the bushes and trees so no one would see them.

In the hut, the poachers were still talking loudly. Apparently, they were still celebrating their successes. Tom, the chief ranger, guided Timbu behind a huge tree. Placing his hand on Timbu's back, he forced him gently down, and said, "Sit, sit and be still." Timbu, sensing that they were after the poachers, sat quietly.

The game wardens circled the hut cautiously and quietly then rushed into the hut and pounced upon the unsuspecting half-intoxicated poachers. There was a scuffle. One of the evil men escaped. He ran behind the giant tree where Timbu was hiding. He had a loaded riffle in his hand. As the game wardens cautiously stepped out of the hut, looking for the escaped man, the armed bandit raised his riffle, with his right index finger pressing slowly on the trigger.

Without a moment's hesitation, and with no thought of danger to himself, Timbu lounged at the man, and struck out at him with his little trunk. The riffle fell to the ground. As the poacher tried to recover his riffle, Timbu stepped on the man's hand and planted his broad hoof on it. This allowed the wardens sufficient time to make an arrest. The hunters were handcuffed and placed in a waiting jeep.

The game wardens went to Timbu. "Thank you little one. Little one, we'll call you Timbu. Thank you Timbu. You saved our lives. What a brave little fellow you are! Now, you too are safe from those evil men. And now we must take you to find your parents." It was Tom who spoke to Timbu.

The wardens walked Timbu deep into the woods. The forest was alive with life. There were birds singing, insects buzzing, lizards scampering, and mountain doves cooing. In the distance, Timbu recognized Simba, his sister, his mom and dad. But it was Simba who ran to Timbu first. Then Timbu's parents came and wrapped their trunks around Timbu's neck. Tears streamed from their eyes. They were so happy to be reunited. For the first time Timbu felt loved and he too cried openly.

Tom said to the elephants. "See I bring you Timbu, our hero. He saved all our lives. "Timbu, dear little Timbu, you are a real hero!" said his father. "You

whom we felt were weak and useless. Please forgive us," said his mother tenderly.

Timbu was moved to tears. Then his mother asked, "Do you suppose that those bad men shot at us because we destroyed the trees and the forest?" "No, mama," said Timbu. "They did it out of greed, but it won't hurt if we all feed on the low shrubs and grasses, and take care of those big beautiful trees. They do shelter us in time of danger and they also provide shelter for our feathered friends."

Timbu, the tiny elephant became the most famous and respected elephant in the herd. From then on, no one dared poke fun at him; nor did they consider him weak anymore. They waited on him, and listened to him whenever he spoke. His mom, dad and Simba had a special place in their heart for him, and in turn, he loved and respected them dearly, especially Simba, for whom he had a tender spot in his big, kind and loving heart.

The Magic Kingdom

In a far-away land lived an evil king named Gantu. His palace was called Doomsday because no one who entered it ever came out alive.

As a little boy, Gantu was the cutest son any parent could desire. His real name then was Benito. Benito's mother, Queen Emily had died in childbirth leaving her maid Stella, a faithful, loving, and loyal lady to care for Prince Benito.

King Danzil, Prince Benito's father had long suspected that an old witch named Akima had something to do with his dear wife's death. As a result, King Danzil made several attempts to rid his kingdom of this evil witch, Akima, but so far he was unsuccessful.

One lovely evening, as the sun began to sink slowly in the West, Stella took Young Prince Benito for a stroll in the palace Garden. The little prince who was only six at the time enjoyed evening walks like most little children do.

King Danzil's kingdom extended for miles around. There were well-kept orchards with fruit trees of every kind. Flower beds with the most exquisite flowering plants dotted the landscape. Floating daintily in the ponds were white water lilies, on which rested nimbly a host of beautiful butterflies including Monarchs, Tiger Swallowtails, Red Admirals, and Mourning Cloaks. At the bottom of the clear-water ponds were many shining coins, which visitors had tossed in while making their favorite wishes. A little bubbly stream with crystal clear water was the home of many colorful fishes that darted here and there. Narrow paths wound around huge trees to allow free movements of pedestrians. On this enchanted evening of this particular day, the weather was perfect for a long stroll. The wind blew soft and gently. Leaves shimmered and danced in the cool breeze. Birds whistled merrily and chirped as they darted from one branch to another.

The evening was so beautiful that it encouraged Stella to keep on walking. Indeed, everything they saw seemed to grip their attention. Stella pointed out several interesting things to the young prince; who was as keen to learn, as she was eager to teach. She kept on walking as though in the grip of some strange magnetic force, and seemed to have lost all sense of time. Soon the evening sun dipped behind the trees and night descended swiftly, and darkness enveloped the whole area.

In the evening gloom, maid Stella became lost. Suddenly in the far distance, she could see the dim light of a flickering wick. This must be the way to the castle, she thought. Little Prince Benito was quite scared, as he was not used to walking in the dark. He clutched Stella's hand and held on to it tightly. "Don't worry little prince Benito, we'll soon be home." She said in an effort to appease his fear.

Unfortunately, little did Stella realize that she was heading in the direction of Akima's home. Akima, the feared, wicked witch was horrible to look at. Everyone in King Danzil's Kingdom was terrified of her. Anyone who mistakenly got too close to her shack was never heard of again. Her evil reputation had spread far and wide. Thus, people tended to avoid passing where she lived, and everyone kept as far away as possible from her.

It was known that Akima, the feared witch, had kidnapped a young seven-year old girl, whom she named Petra and forced her to live with her. This pretty little girl was stolen from a young couple who had wandered near Akima's home. Akima was raising Petra as her own daughter. This would ensure that she had a successor who would continue to carry out her wicked designs.

Akima had long envied young Prince Benito, because he was so very handsome. His long curly locks drooped over his shoulders and shone like gold in the sunshine. She particularly hated the young Prince because he resembled his father. And he reminded her of the king, whom she despised passionately, because he was trying to get rid of her. Every time Akima thought about King Danzil, she became enraged and vowed that she will get even with him. "One day I surely will!" She had promised.

Meanwhile, Stella had unsuspectingly wandered too close to Akima's home. She thought that the light she was following came from the king's castle. Imagine her great surprise when she heard the words: "Hello... Stella!

Hello...Little Prince Benito! Ha! Ha! Ha! Looking for me I suppose. I see you have come to pay me a visit. Welcome! Welcome! Ha! Ha! Ha! Don't just stand there. Come in! Come in! Ha! Ha! Ha!"

Without a moment's hesitation, Akima grabbed Stella's hand and pulled her roughly into her house dragging little Prince Benito, who was holding on to maid Stella's hand for dear life behind her. "Yes, yes, I have l-o-n-g waited for this MOMENT!" She stamped her feet. "Let King DANZIL save you now! I hate him! O, how I hate him! You shall see! You shall see!"

Poor Stella and Prince Benito were scared to death. They trembled and shook uncontrollably. Their knees almost buckled under their weight. Their faces became ghastly pale and as white as ghosts. Their eyes stared widely into open space. "You both look nervous, but I have just the right thing for you." Said Akima in a gruff voice. It will surely calm you down. Ha! Ha! Ha!" Her wicked, raspy voice crackled menacingly.

Akima had a magic potion which she called "Potion Reverso." It had the strange power to change anything into its opposite - good people became evil, small things became big, beautiful things turned ugly, kind-hearted people became cruel and wicked, the young turned old, and the old became young again. This was the drink Akima had offered them to take.

Petra, Akima's adopted daughter felt very sorry for Stella and especially for the little prince. Petra had a kind and gentle heart. She always openly disapproved of Akima's wicked ways. "Mother, must you do that? Please mother spare them, please mother, not again. Leave them alone." Petra sobbed aloud.

In a rage, Akima pushed her away. "Get away from me you little tramp!" "Let me be, let me be." Poor Petra slumped quietly behind a chair and wept. There was nothing she could do. "Come here now! Petra! Do you hear me?" Akima grabbed Petra by the shoulders and shook her forcefully. "Look, you little monster, don't ever meddle in my affairs. Understand! Now go outside and play with the wolves!" She dragged her out of the house and slammed the door shut.

Petra had witnessed many strange happenings in the past. She had repeated nightmares about them. On such occasions, if she caused Akima to wake up, the wicked witch would slap her until she cried herself to sleep. Akima did this, because she wanted Petra to become as evil as she. Sometimes in the middle of the night when Petra knew that Akima was asleep, she got down on her knees and prayed to her Guardian Angel. She always hid when she prayed so that Akima would not see her, as this would spell disaster for her.

Now Akima took some of the magic potion and poured it in a glass. She gave some of the drink to Stella and the rest to Prince Benito. It had a sweetish smell. "Here Stella, if you wish to return to the castle, you and Benito must drink. Now open your mouths." Stella was too scared to refuse, or to do otherwise. In any event, Akima would have shoved it down her throat. So Stella and the little prince drank the liquid. Instantly, they both fell into a deep sleep, and when they awoke early next morning, they were no longer the same persons they were before they drank Akima's potion.

Meanwhile back at the Castle all night long, the king's guard searched the palace grounds, the garden and just about everywhere. They found no trace of maid Stella and Prince Benito.

At Akima's home Prince Benito had been transformed into an old man. He had a full-grown beard and deeply furrowed brow. He had dark cruel lines on his face, and a stern look. His manners were crude and rough. Akima with a wicked grin on her withered face said teasingly, "Hello King Gantu!

Your name is now King Gantu; you are no longer Prince Benito. Remember, King Gantu, you can now return to your castle." She pointed the way to the castle. "Ha! Ha! Ha!" and laughed a wicked witch's laugh.

As for the maid, Stella she had been transformed into an ugly and mischievous girl. Her hair was wildly ragged and her dress was in tatters. She ran around wildly and behaved like a spoilt brat. Akima laughed loudly, screamed with delight and amusement, and teased poor Stella. "Hi Stellito, that's your new name." "Stellito and King Gantu, Ha, Ha! Ha! There's the road to your castle. King Danzil is waiting on you. Now, get out! Get out!" She pushed them out the door.

King Gantu had to chase wildly after Stellito who rolled on the ground and stamped on his feet. This enraged King Gantu so much that he dragged her all the way to the castle. He mumbled strange noises, grumbled, got angry fussed and fumed over every thing.

Two guards who were sent in search of Stella and Prince Benito, saw these two strange figures emerging from the shadows of Akima's home. Instantly they knew that the evil witch had cast a spell on the prince and Stella. The castle was very well protected and no stranger ever wandered aimlessly in the garden. They also knew that Akima hated King Danzil and would stop at nothing to get even with him for banishing her from his kingdom. Therefore, the guards ran ahead and told King Danzil what they had seen and warned him of their coming.

When King Gantu reached the castle, he shouted and ordered the guards and the servants into the prison and locked them up. He acted as a raging bull. He rushed madly at his father who tried to escape. Stellito was highly amused. She laughed uproariously, and giggled annoyingly. King Danzil instantly knew that Witch Akima was responsible for this outrageous behaviour of his son Benito, who now called himself King Gantu, and maid Stella, who now answered to the name Stellito.

Poor King Danzil promptly left the castle to seek help for his son and his maid. But he had to seek refuge elsewhere, because he feared for his life. Yet he vowed to get even with Akima one day.

As time went by, King Gantu grew worse. Visitors who chanced to go by or anyone who dared to enter the castle was never heard of again. He had them imprisoned for life. Thus the castle became known as Doomsday. In fact no one knew for certain what actually went on there. From time to time, Stellito's loud shrieks could be heard coming from within. Sometimes she got King Gantu so angry, because of her naughty antics, that on several occasions, he had to tie her up.

Many years went by. At Akima's house, Petra had grown into a young woman. She had that sad and far-away look in her eyes like most abused children do. She mistrusted her so-called mother. Deep down Petra resented Akima for her evil ways. Silently she longed to help restore Prince Benito and Stella to their former selves, yet Petra felt powerless. Old, hideous Akima was ever watchful; and Petra dared not go into King Gantu's castle for fear that she would never return alive.

At every available opportunity Petra, even as a child when chasing butterflies, would quietly speak to her Guardian Angel. She would say, "Pretty little butterflies, how I wish I were like you. You do not have a cruel witch to call mother. Look how you float about so daintily. Maybe you can reach my Guardian Angel and speak to her for me. If I were like you, I would surely fly away and go as far away as possible from my wicked witch mother Akima, whom I hope I would never see again."

One night after praying and crying herself to sleep, Petra fell into a deep trance-like sleep. She dreamt that her Guardian Angel had visited her. The Angel who was more beautiful than anyone Petra had ever seen, spoke to her in a soft and tender voice." My dearest Petra, you will soon be released from Akima, this vile, old witch. Then you must go and save Prince Benito and Maid Stella from the witch's spell. But first, you must do the following: Waste no time."

"You must pretend to be very tired when Akima comes into your room in the morning. She will do everything possible to try and wake you up. Keep still. Keep your eyes shut tightly. She would pinch and slap you but pretend that you do not feel anything. Be brave! Akima, thinking that you are too tired to get up, will go outside to tend to her garden. When you hear her fussing outside, get out of bed quickly."

The Angel continued, "Go into the kitchen cupboard. There you will see three vials each containing a dusty coloured powder. When mixed together, they have the power to dissolve or make anyone, or anything disappear completely. Pour them into one vial and mix them thoroughly. Return to your bed and pretend to be fast asleep."

"Akima will come into your room to wake you up. She would be really mad at you because you are still asleep. She will bend over you to rip the covers off you. At that precise moment, act as though you have awakened in a fright. Swing your hand and spray the powder in her face. She will collapse instantly. Then return to the kitchen and you will see the magic potion, which she gave Stella and Prince Benito. Add some white vinegar to it. This neutralizes the potion and reverses the effect. You must then try to give some to King Gantu and Stellito."

Petra said to her Guardian Angel, "How will I be able to administer this anti-potion to them. If I were to enter the castle I would be imprisoned or killed." "Never fear my child. The three coloured powders, green, yellow and red when combined are deadly, but used separately they have different effects. The yellow powder makes you become invisible. The red powder paralyzes its victim. But, the green powder can restore the victim back to health. "Now do as I say, and peace be with you, dear Petra." And the Angel departed.

Morning broke, and Petra did exactly as the Angel had told her. When Akima returned from tending her garden, and found Petra still sleeping, she was furious. "You, good-for-nothing! You lazy tramp. I am trying to raise you like myself. I think I have made a mistake. Now get up! Get up!" She yelled at Petra. Akima bent over, reached for the covers and was about to rip the covers off Petra, when Petra with one sudden swing of her hand let fly the powder-mixture in Akima's face. With a piercing shriek, “Eeeek, Aaaaa!” Akima collapsed and crumbled in a heap on the floor. Her body dissolved and burnt into cinders, leaving a small puff of smoke.

Petra still trembling with fright from this fearful ordeal climbed out of bed and went to the kitchen where she neutralized the potion. Then taking the three different-coloured powders, which her Guardian Angel had directed her to take with her, she immediately set out for the castle.

Petra's heart beat wildly with excitement and expectation as she approached the castle. She looked everywhere but saw no one. She ran into the King's huge garden and was surprised to see the wonderful plants and the landscaping. Though the garden was unattended, much of it was still very beautiful. She passed through the orchard, the lily pond, the clear stream and the tall, stately plants and soon found herself in front of the castle.

There Petra stood facing the giant front door of the castle. She was scared, but was determined to enter the castle. She was thinking about how she might be able to get in without arousing the suspicion of the wicked king. But this thought was short-lived for in an instant, she heard a booming voice.
"Stop there! You, whoever you are!" The door flung open. Without a moment's hesitation, Petra whizzed through the open door. King Gantu rushed headlong after her shouting, "You crazy woman! What do you want?
You 're not welcome here! Get out! Get out before I rip you apart!"

Petra sprinkled the yellow powder on herself. Instantly she became invisible. King Gantu lashed out this way and that. He was infuriated. He stamped his feet so hard that they almost crashed through the floor. He scowled, growled and clenched his fist. He thumped his chest loudly and shouted obscenities. Crazy Stellito grinned at him and mocked him. He dashed after her, grabbed her by the hair, twisted her neck and stared into her upturned face. Petra sprinkled herself with the green powder and became visible again. She was standing five feet from the wall.

King Gantu released Stellito who howled with laughter, and rushed madly after her. Petra then used the yellow powder and again became invisible causing King Gantu to crash into the wall and fall to the ground. Petra immediately sprinkled him with the red powder. This paralyzed him temporarily. Naughty Stellito ran to King Gantu to poke fun at him. Petra seized the opportunity to sprinkle the red powder on Stellito as well. She too became immobile.

Petra then gave them both, King Gantu and Stellito sips of the anti-potion. Magically, King Gantu became Benito again, now transformed into a dashing, young handsome prince, and ugly Stellito regained Stella's natural beauty and calm demeanor. The Prince looked at Petra. Instantly, he recognized her as the girl who lived with the wicked Akima, and who had pleaded with the witch to save their lives. "Thank you, young maiden. You are a heroine!" As their eyes met, Petra's stunning beauty and grace overwhelmed the

Prince. Petra was exceedingly impressed with Benito's handsome features and his gentle manners, and they fell instantly in love. "You have saved my life sweet maiden. Now will you be my bride?" "Indeed, fine Sir, I will, I will," responded Petra.

Maid Stella unlocked the cells. Guards, maids, servants, butlers, gardeners, visitors to the Royal Palace and officials staggered out. They were thin and sickly looking, but very relieved. They thanked Stella, and especially Petra, again and again for what she had done.

News of the prisoners' release and that normalcy had returned to the palace spread quickly throughout the kingdom as visitors reached their families. A very important event was unfolding.

In the distance, a figure on horseback was seen galloping slowly to the palace. It was King Danzil. A messenger had been sent to let him know that his palace was now safe for his return. On arriving he greeted Stella, and thanked Petra for ridding the Kingdom of the wicked witch. He hugged his son and gave his blessing to Prince Benito and his future daughter-in-law, Petra. In addition, he also made them rulers over his kingdom.

Shortly after King Danzil's return to the castle, Prince Benito and Petra were married in a lavish ceremony. King Danzil escorted Petra to the altar and gave her to his son. There was never a more beautiful and happy marriage. Such great merriment had never been witnessed in the Palace before. Everyone was joyful. There was much love and happiness among the guests, and peace and contentment filled the newly-weds.

Before the guests had all departed, the smiling Prince announced that he had a special present for his bride. She was thrilled, and wondered what this present might be. She had already received the most exquisite diamond ring. But never in her wildest dreams did she expect to see her live biological parents, whom she thought were long dead, standing before her. She hugged them ever so tightly and kissed them. Then turning to her husband, she planted a long and loving kiss on his cheek for this very precious gift.

The handsome Prince and his beautiful Princess reigned happily, justly and contentedly over the people in his kingdom. There was much peace and good will and their subjects loved them very dearly. The dramatic change in peoples' mood in the kingdom was so stunning that the original name of MAGIC KINGDOM was restored to their castle home forever.

GROUP II
SHORT STORIES

THE CASE OF THE SINGLE PEARL

Mrs. Emily Currie lived with her retired husband Henry in an affluent neighborhood in the suburbs of Toronto. The Curries had no children. Their home was an old, but expensive brick mansion- a sprawling, two-floor building. It nestled cozily on a corner lot. Climbing ivy clung desperately to the brick walls; masking with its green leaves the grey texture, which was now less evident.

Everyone in the neighbourhood knew the Curries were wealthy. A shining, red Porsche 924, the latest model was parked in the long driveway. Emily Currie, now greying and in her early sixties, was always elegantly dressed. Her exquisitely designed jewellery matched and complemented every outfit.

Robert, a youthful and handsome sixteen- year old, regularly delivered a copy of the daily newspaper, "The Globe and Mail", to the Currie's home. Robert was a courteous, sensitive and caring lad. Rob, as he was familiarly called, lived in a poor overcrowded neighbourhood that bordered the suburb in which the Curries lived. He was no stranger to the Curries.

On several occasions, he was called on to do little odd jobs in and around the house. There was that time when the house-cleaner was ill; Mrs. Currie gave him the job to clean the windows. The Curries had a special liking for Rob, particularly Emily. Indeed, in the cold of winter, she would often invite him into the house to join her for hot apple cider or hot chocolate, since her home was usually the last one on his paper route.

As far as Rob was concerned, the Curries were wealthy, but they were kind and generous. They paid him handsomely for anything he did for them. Yet, it bothered him when he compared their lifestyle with those wretched poor in his neighbourhood. He could never dismiss from his mind the family who had plastic covering over their windows to keep out the cold because they could not afford to fix the broken window- panes. Their children having very little to eat, were always hungry. The scant and tattered clothing on their scrawny backs were all they had to keep them warm. Nor could he dismiss from his mind the other very poor family of four who lived only a couple of blocks from his home. They could only afford to share a single room. They slept on the floor with discarded newspapers for a mattress. An empty, battered refrigerator and a couple wooden boxes for seats comprised all their possessions.

On this pleasant fall day in early October, Rob set out on his rounds to deliver The Globe and Mail. The strikingly rich, fall colours of red, gold, orange and purple leaves dotted the landscape and made it an artist's paradise. The touch of Nature's autumn brought on those cool, invigorating and nostalgic breezes. Emily and Henry had left for the Royal Alexandra Theatre in downtown Toronto to enjoy a performance of The Phantom of the Opera.

It was about seven-thirty in the evening. Rob had just about completed his rounds collecting the money for his daily newspapers. As usual, his final stop was at the "Curries.' As Rob approached the house, he noticed the absence of the Porsche. The garage door was closed. The gate was bolted on the inside, but there was no padlock in the metal ring. He gained entry to the grounds by unbolting the gate. He had done this many times before. On such occasions Mrs. Currie would say quite casually, "Rob, just unbolt the gate and come in." Today, when Rob entered the premises and knocked on the door, there was no answer. He knocked again and again, but still there was no answer. He was sure the Curries were not at home.

Robert felt his heart pounding madly in his chest. It raced wildly, at times skipping a beat or two. At that moment, he felt the urge to get hold of a piece of Mrs. Currie's jewels. His intention was to sell it and distribute all the proceeds to those poor, unfortunate souls in his neighbourhood. 'After all, what's just one piece? Mrs. Currie would never miss it.' He rationalized. In any event, he was certain that the Curries would never suspect him of committing an offence like theft.

Robert, now totally absorbed with this outrageous idea, seemed to have lost control of himself. The thought of helping the poor seemed just the right thing to do. It consumed his entire being, and impaired and blunted his reasoning. He focused his mind particularly on old Luther, the poor crippled beggar, who hobbled about and slept in alleyways. Very few people ever took any notice of his helpless condition and his disability.

Rob recalled looking at episodes of the made-for-T.V. movie, 'Robin Hood'. The hero, Robin Hood had similar motives. He robbed the rich to give to the poor. Rob felt that indeed this was a noble thing to do, and worthy of emulating. Rob was sure the Curries would not return in a hurry. Sticking out of the mailbox was a note. It read, "Rob, we've gone to the theatre, see you tomorrow, I'll pay you then."

Without wasting any time, Robert went to the rear of the house. He turned the handle of the kitchen door gently, not knowing what to expect. Surprisingly, it yielded. It was not the first time that the Curries had forgotten to secure this back door. They had lived there for well over thirty years, and there had never been any attempt to burglarize their home. With an advanced security system installed in the house, they felt very safe in this upscale neighbourhood.

Rob gently pushed the door open and entered cautiously. He was careful not to set off the alarm. He knew where the wires were. On several occasions when he was invited in the house, Mrs. Currie would often caution him. "Rob, step over here, be careful you don't trip on the wire. It will trigger the alarm." Rob headed straight for the master bedroom. This room was neat and richly decorated. Expensive lace curtains draped every window. A framed masterpiece hung opposite the brass-framed canopied bed. The antique, mahogany wardrobe, artistically engraved was polished to a glittering shine. However, what attracted Rob's attention was none of these, but the jewel box. It sat comfortably on the dresser staring at him. It beckoned him invitingly, and he took the bait.

Rob reached for the jewel box with eager expectation. His hands trembled and cold sweat beaded his forehead. He nervously raised the lid to reveal a rich assortment of handcrafted jewels and a collection of other rare gems- the likes of which Rob had never seen.

This collection must be worth a fortune, he thought. Rob examined the diamond pendants, the emerald ring, the large opal, but his gaze became transfixed on a single pearl. It was one of the most beautiful and exquisite trinkets he had ever seen. 'This must be priceless, it will fetch a good price." He thought to himself. Its uniqueness and striking beauty captivated him.

With trembling hands, and rapid breathing, he anxiously took hold of it ever so gently. He held the pearl between his thumb and index finger, and began to roll and admire it. The pearl felt smooth to the touch. After admiring it, and thinking how many poor people could benefit from the money he could fetch from its sale, he attempted to put it into his pocket.

To his utter dismay, the pearl accidentally slipped through his fingers and rolled somewhere under the bed. He immediately dropped down on all fours thinking there was no way he would leave without this valuable pearl. Lowering his head under the bed, and straining his eyes to see in the dim light, he beheld what appeared to be the pearl under the bed. Desperately, he tried to reach it, when suddenly and unexpectedly he heard a noise coming from the direction of the front door, as though someone was opening it.

The Curries had forgotten their tickets on the triple dresser, and had returned prematurely to retrieve them. On their way to the theatre, Henry had asked his wife. "Honey, do you have the tickets?" Emily opened her purse and ran her fingers through it only to discover that she had forgotten them on the dresser.

The Curries did not expect to find anyone at home of course, nor did they suspect that there was an intruder in their house. They entered and closed the door behind them. Rob heard the door slam. His heart pounded furiously. There was no time to think. There was no place to hide. "Under no circumstance must I be seen." He heard himself saying. Instinctively, he ran to the window. He quickly opened it without making any noise. Like a frightened rabbit, he hopped through the open window. Fortunately for him, the window was not very high off the ground. His knees buckled under his weight as he jumped to the ground and he managed to crawl behind some ornamental bushes nearby. There he hid.

The Curries entered the master bedroom. It looked no different from the way they had left it. Nothing seemed to have been disturbed. Emily said, "Henry, there's a draft coming in. Don't tell me that you forgot to close the window." Henry looked puzzled. "Maybe I did, Hon., but I am sure that I closed it as I always did. I guess, I must be more careful the next time." He went towards the window to shut it. "OH, here they are dear!" "What?" asked Henry. "The tickets of course, just where I left them. Let's hurry so we won't be late."

After a short while Rob heard the Curries drive off. He felt almost faint with the stress of the moment as he thought, “What if that sweet lady had caught me stealing!” He felt sick to his stomach. He thought about his senseless action and mumbled to himself. “How stupid can I be? How can I give what I don’t have? In attempting to solve one problem, I am creating an even bigger one. This is folly! Yes, I got carried away with this insane idea. What a poor fool I am.” Rob cautiously left his hiding place and left the Currie’s property, quietly closing the gate behind him as he left.

All night long Rob tossed in bed as he replayed the events of the evening in his mind. Every time he thought about what might have occurred if he had been caught, his heart skipped beats and raced wildly as he broke into a cold sweat. When morning dawned, he avoided speaking to anyone. “Rob,” said his mother, “You are so quiet. Is something the matter?” “No mom, I’m just tired.” He had nothing for breakfast. “Too tired to eat something for breakfast Rob?” His mom asked. He had that worried look as though he was haunted by something dreadful. He smiled sheepishly at his mother, took up his books and left for school.

After school, Rob went about his business delivering papers. He was not his buoyant self. His guilt gnawed inside him. He became sullen and distraught when he reached the Curries'. He was shaking visibly. He kept repeating to himself. "I didn't do this for myself. I wouldn't do anything to hurt that sweet lady. God knows how I feel." "Rob, did you get the note I left in the mailbox?" inquired Mrs. Currie. "Yes Mrs. C." "What's the matter Rob? You don't seem yourself today," continued Mrs. Currie. Rob tried to avoid looking her directly in the eyes. "I'm O.K. Mrs. C."

Mrs. Currie paid Rob in cash for the week's supply of papers and gave him a generous tip, adding, "This is for all your kindness Rob." Then Mrs. Currie said in a pleasant voice, "Would you please come in for a minute Rob, I have something important to discuss with you." Mrs. Currie was her usual kind self. She treated him no differently than any other occasion. "I'm in a hurry today, Mrs. C," Rob replied. "Well, Rob, this won't take that long," said Mrs. Currie, "Please come in."

They entered by the front door. Rob held the door to allow Mrs. Currie to go ahead of him. She motioned him to sit at the kitchen table. "Would you have a glass of apple juice, or orange?" "Orange, please." She gave him a glass of orange juice and sat next to him. Rob was certain that she knew nothing of that fateful evening. Yet, he felt very uncomfortable. He was nervous, but Mrs. Currie appeared to dismiss his nervousness as anxiety to get home quickly.

Mrs. Currie looked at Rob rather condescendingly. "Rob, I couldn't help observing the poverty in your neighbourhood over the years. It has always grieved me to see those homeless victims, the wayward beggars. There must be some way I can be of help to them. We have a few days left before Thanksgiving Day. Indeed I've so much to be thankful for." While talking to him, her hand involuntary went to her necklace. She played with the diamond pendant with her fingers.

"Look, I have an idea. Tell me what you think of it!" She seemed all excited. "Know what Rob, I think I will sell a piece of my jewellery. You can have the money to distribute among the poor in your neighbourhood. You know them better than I do." Rob was dumbfounded. "Just what I had in mind," he thought. He became terribly excited, and for a moment, he forgot his latest escapade. "Yes, I think that's a brilliant idea, Mrs. C." "Good then. Let's go into my bedroom. That's where I keep my jewel box. It's too heavy for me to bring all the way into the kitchen. I want you to help me choose the piece, Rob."

Rob followed Mrs. Currie into the bedroom. Henry, her husband was reading the daily newspaper in the family room. "Hello Mr. Currie." "Hi Rob," Henry replied without raising his head from behind the newspaper. "Henry, do you remember what we discussed earlier today? Well, I'm going to let Rob help me choose," Mrs. Currie said as she and Rob made their way into the master bedroom.

Mrs. Currie opened her jewel box. It was filled with the finest gems. She took out one piece at a time and studied each carefully. She seemed to be looking for something special. Then she paused and looking straight at Rob, she said. "You know Rob, I'm certain I have this rare pearl. It is very costly. Henry bought it for me when we were vacationing in Australia. I was going to have it mounted on a ring; but I have so many rings. Some I never wear. I was thinking of selling it and distributing the proceeds among the poor in your neighbourhood. "Come closer Rob, your eyes are better than mine. Look carefully. I am certain it is there. I am the only one who ever opens my jewel box."

"I don't see it anywhere, Mrs. C. Maybe you can sell another piece," Robert responded. "I suppose I can," said Mrs. Currie. "Could it have fallen out when you took out another piece, Mrs. Currie?" Robert said. "That's possible Rob, but highly unlikely, for I haven't taken anything out from that box for a very long time. As a matter-of fact I seldom ever do, because I keep the ones I use regularly on top of the box, so I can have easy access to them when I need to use one. I wonder, where could it have fallen?" inquired Mrs. Currie.

"It is smooth to the touch, isn't it, Mrs. C.? Perhaps it could have rolled under the bed, Mrs. C." I can't think of anyplace else where it could possibly be," interjected Robert. "Will you please look under the bed for me Rob? Here's a flashlight." Rob bent down on all four limbs. He peered under the bed just where he knew the pearl had fallen from his fingers. There staring at him was the singularly lovely pearl. "I do see something. Yes, I think it is the pearl," said Robert in a tremulous voice. "Well, what are you waiting for? Pick it up Rob, pick it up," replied Mrs. Currie. Rob's fingers shook so nervously that he had difficulty holding on to it. Its smoothness did not allow him to grasp it easily. "Here it is," he said. "Rob, your hands, look at how they're shaking." "It's the pearl, it is so beautiful!" Rob said, his voice trembling with emotion. He was trying very hard to fight back his guilt, but his looks betrayed him. He looked scared like a frightened rabbit.

Mrs. Currie remembered the open window. She looked at Rob with sadness in her eyes. "You knew how it got there. Didn't you, Rob?" There was silence. Rob felt very uneasy, and thought, "How can I tell this sweet lady that I was the one." He felt very uncomfortable and guilty. He lowered his head and mumbled something incoherently under his breadth. "Yes, Rob?" she looked at him encouragingly. Tears flowed freely from Rob's eyes. He shook uncontrollably. He was sick and pale with remorse. "Mrs. C." He choked on the words. He buried his hands in his face and said, "I'm so very sorry, Mrs. C. I don't know what came over me. I thought only of the starving poor. I'm sorry, I'm so very sorry." Rob broke down and sobbed like a baby.

Mrs. Currie looked at Rob and in a stern voice said. "Now you listen to me Rob. What you did was unpardonable. I love you like a son. We have always trusted you like family. Now what am I to make of this?" She stared at him again. She read the look of despair in his eyes, the remorse, the hurt, and the disappointment. Again, she continued in the same tone of voice. Rob had never seen her like this before. She was always smiling and calm. How different she seemed. Her countenance took on that look of scorn. Yet, beneath it, there was something compellingly sweet.

"Rob, during these past years that I've known you, you've been there for us. You were honest and straightforward." She paused. She distinctly recalled the time when he had finished cleaning her car. He came waving a $20 bill informing her in an excited voice, "Mrs. C, I found it under your car seat." Another time, she mistakenly gave him a $100 bill for a $2 note. He returned it promptly saying, "Mrs. C., you made a mistake." She was convinced that he would not steal for himself.

"You can get yourself into serious trouble for this. Your good reputation would be tarnished forever," she said sternly. Rob lowered his head and shut his eyes. "Mrs. Currie, I deserved to be punished. Do what you have to do." He didn't look her in the face. He was too embarrassed and ashamed of his senseless behaviour. "Didn't you think of asking me Rob?" she chided. After a long period of silence in which she seemed to be studying him, she added in a stern voice, "Rob, I want you to remember what I am going to say to you, as long as you live."

"Rob, noble intentions ought to be characterized by worthy deeds. In life, it's not only what you do that matters, but also how it is done. Not just what you say, but also how it is said. You must always be guided by a set of principles, and the motives for which action is taken ought to be based upon valued judgments. You should never try to correct an injustice or an evil deed by performing a corresponding evil action. Two wrongs never make a right. To make this world a better place in which to live, you must take a positive approach, apply the most logical and appropriate solutions to all problems and involve God in all your plans. He will never let you down, and you will never go wrong in whatever you do."

Having said this, Mrs. Currie concluded by saying, "Rob, please come by tomorrow. I'll have the money ready for you. Make sure that it is distributed to the needy before Thanksgiving Day." With tears streaming from his eyes, Rob thanked her. "I love you Mrs. C. Please forgive my indiscretion." "You're forgiven, Rob," she replied, " but remember that it takes only one serious mistake

to ruin one's good reputation and sometimes one's life."
Robert left the Currie's a wiser and more prudent lad.

CALLABAN

On a spreading two hundred acres cattle and sheep farm lived Joel and his beautiful wife Sarah. Joel was a robust and rugged individual of thirty-four. Sarah was a slightly built woman in her late twenties. They had been married for five years and had no children.

A couple of Ranch hands, whom Joel had hired, worked on the farm. They performed a number of chores which included tending to the cattle and sheep. Joel however, relied heavily on a team of seven specially trained dogs. Their main task was to care for the cattle and sheep, by rounding them up when the day was done, and ensuring that they were safe at all times.

Other farmers in the neighbourhood complained of losses from predators like wolves, but not Joel. In fact, he had never lost one head of cattle or a single sheep. He attributed this feat mainly to his dedicated team of skilled dogs that worked tirelessly to safeguard his herd of cattle and his flock of sheep.

Among Joel's team of highly trained dogs, was this special dog, Callaban, whose father was a Wolfhound and his mother a Collie. He had the wild, shaggy and ferocious look of his father, but the kind and gentle disposition of his mother. Callaban wasn't just any ordinary dog. Indeed, he was greatly devoted to Joel, his master, and also to Sarah, his mistress. He had always shown signs of sincere affection and faithfulness to them. What impressed Joel most about this dog was the serious manner with which he went about his daily tasks. Callaban was thoroughly dedicated to his duties and he was a real leader. At the end of the day, Callaban was always the very last one to get home, because he would make it his duty to see that every sheep, heifer, bull or calf was accounted for on the farm. Indeed, he would go to any extreme to see that this was the case. Thus, he would always return to the field after all the other dogs had returned to make a final round to ensure that every sheep or cattle was safely home.

Callaban was really an effective leader. If one of the other dogs strayed from the team, delayed in the performance of its duties, or was too playful in rounding up the sheep, Callaban would get after it. He would bark, nudge or nip the offending culprit. His yelps reminded the slacker that there was a job to be done. Nor would he leave that particular offending dog until it rejoined the team and continued to tend to the business on hand.

When Callaban was done for the day, he would enter his master's house, proudly wagging his bushy tail. He snuggled up to Joel and rested his shaggy head in the palms of Joel's hands. At such times, Joel would run his coarse hands along Callaban's back. He would hold him by the scruff of his neck, and shake him in a friendly manner, to indicate how pleased he was with him. Callaban would then brush past Sarah's long skirt. He would stop and look at her with a childish glint in his eyes. She would give him a reassuring pat on his head saying, "Good boy, Callaban!" Then she would feed him his favorite meal.

Once during a wild winter storm, rounding up the stock had become particularly difficult. It was very tedious work. Joel and his farm labourers worked tirelessly to secure the entire stock of animals. The storm raged all day long. Snow drifted and piled high against stumps of trees now bare of leaves. The temperature plummeted and the wind chill factor reached record lows at the end of the day. Joel and his farm workers retired to their quarters to seek refuge from the biting cold. They were certain that the dogs would take care of the rest.

As was his custom, Callaban took a final look around, and it was during this time that he noticed a heifer straying far off in the distance. She was almost out of sight. He knew that she did not have a chance to survive in this extreme cold if she did not enter the barn. She would certainly freeze to death. Callaban went after her. He struggled against the huge snowdrifts, as he was determined to save her from a painful death.

Meanwhile, the other dogs had reached home and were being fed, all except Callaban. The storm's fury worsened. Joel pushed the door slightly ajar. The force of the blinding storm closed it instantly. He pushed at it with all his might and shouted at the top of his voice, "Callaban! Callaban!" He heard nothing. He saw nothing. He uttered a piercing whistle. It was the one that Callaban responded to instantly. Again, there was no response.

Joel put on his heaviest coat. He took a lantern and went outside hoping to spot Callaban. He again whistled and shouted the dog's name. There was still no sign of his favorite dog. Joel felt desperate and worried. He knew it was a waste of time to try to locate Callaban in the blinding snowdrifts. In any event, he himself couldn't go very far in this fierce storm.

Joel turned and was about to get into his house when he heard slushing noises. He spun around involuntarily. Straining his eyes in the darkness, he barely discerned two shadowy figures, a slim shivering, frightened heifer closely followed by a snow-coated Callaban whose whiskers were frosted and eyes almost closed from the icicles surrounding them.

Joel ran towards the animals. He rushed the heifer into the barn.

Callaban whined a low familiar growl happy to be home. He wagged his frosted tail now coated heavily with ice. Ice crystals dangled from frozen whiskers. Black, beady eyes peered from between frosty lashes, which made it very difficult to see. Callaban shivered from the long exposure in the intense cold, but he was alive and well. He had just risked his life in the line of duty. Because of his commitment and extra-ordinary efforts in the line of duty, he had saved a heifer's life and he was delighted to have done such a fine job.

Joel and Sarah were thrilled and extremely pleased with his effort, and rewarded him with an extra serving of his favorite meal. Joel was overcome by what Callaban had done and appreciated even more the unusual, valuable and unique qualities of this dog. Callaban seemed to be almost human-like in his concern for other creatures and especially those that belonged to his master. Sarah patted him tenderly and fed him some warm, solid food. Callaban then eagerly lapped up a bowl of warm milk and then curled up by the fireplace, to take a well earned nap.

Several months after this remarkable incident, Sarah gave birth to a beautiful, bouncing baby girl. This baby was Sarah and Joel's first, and they named her Jenny. Joel and Sarah had always longed for a child, so when this new baby came into their lives, they were obviously extremely excited and delighted to have this wonderful new addition to the family. So thrilled were they, that they spent every waking minute attending to baby Jenny. Baby Jenny became the centre of attraction, as is often the case with a newborn baby.

Months went by, and with each passing day, Joel and Sarah became more attached to their dear little infant. They became so intensely preoccupied with her that they had little time for Callaban. Moreover, they fussed over baby Jen to such an extent that if Callaban approached the crib, Joel would yell at him, "Get away from there, Callaban! Don't you ever go near the baby!"

Baby Jen though, liked to play with Callaban. She would smile and put her little fingers for Callaban to lick. When he attempted to playfully kiss baby Jen's finger, Joel would rudely shout at Callaban. "Get away from her Callaban, didn't you hear me!" Callaban never understood what he was doing wrong for he always considered himself an important part of the family.

One day, baby Jenny who was hungry began crying very loudly. Callaban entered the room and stood by the crib to see what was the matter. Joel and Sarah burst into the room and found Callaban standing near the crib peering at baby Jenny, wondering why she was crying. "Callaban!" Shouted Joel angrily. "Didn't I tell you that you should never go near the baby? I am sure that you have scared her, and that's why she is bawling her head off." Now get out! If you ever harm this child, I don't know what I would do to you. I...I would kill you Callaban!" Callaban left the room meekly with his tail trailing between his hind legs.

Thinking that he was part of the family, Callaban could not understand what all the fuss was about, and why his presence near the baby was not acceptable. He felt that it was his duty to protect the baby just as he did the cattle and sheep. He was determined not to be denied this privilege, so he continued to visit baby Jen, whenever the opportunity arose. Gradually Callaban began to realize that no one paid him much attention any more. He felt thoroughly neglected as baby Jenny was receiving all his mistress and master's attention. Yet, this did not seem to bother him that much, and as usual, he went about his business as eagerly and as dutifully as ever.

On one occasion, to show his displeasure at being so neglected, he deliberately went near the crib and whined. Joel threatened him and chased him out of the room. On another occasion, Callaban uttered a sharp bark in a playful manner near the crib to draw baby Jen's attention. Joel was so enraged that, using his hand; he struck Callaban a sharp blow on his back and pushed him out of the room. "Callaban!" He shouted, "Jenny is our baby, no harm must ever come to her. Now get out and stay out!" Callaban had previously observed that objects that were not needed by anyone were often put into the garbage bin. He saw soiled, disposable diapers ending up there. He wondered why his master hadn't thought of throwing him there. After all, he was being treated as garbage.

One day, Callaban saw a dirty diaper at the foot of the crib. He had intended to dispose of it in the garbage bin in the same manner as he had seen Joel and Sarah doing many times before. He innocently reached for it, but his paws got caught in the bars of the crib. The noise of his paws scratching on the crib awoke baby Jenny. She got up in a fright and began to scream.

What a commotion this created! Joel and Sarah rushed into the room and caught Callaban in the act. "Callaban!" Joel yelled, "Didn't I tell you that if you ever touch this child, I will kill you! Now get out!" He shoved Callaban out of the room. The poor dog whimpered and with tears in his eyes left the room as a forsaken child.

Two weeks after this incident, there was a great commotion in the house. Sarah was at her wit's end. "Joel! Joel!" she shouted frantically. "Do you have the baby?" "No!" came the reply. "She is in her crib. Isn't she?" inquired Joel. "No, Joel! She isn't there!" said a sobbing Sarah. Joel rushed into the room. "My God, where can she be? My poor baby!" There was panic on his face.

Joel and Sarah searched everywhere. There was no trace of baby Jenny. Joel was visibly shaken. He rushed outside like a mad man. "Ben! Ben! Have you seen the baby?" He yelled at a farm hand at the top of his voice. "Who?" asked Ben. "Our Baby Jen! Our baby Jen!" "No!" came the reply. "And Ruben, your pal..." "Sir, he has been in the field all day since early dawn," said a dejected Ben. "I will search around the house. Sir, I heard that there is a killer wolf roaming the neighbourhood." Ben rushed off looking everywhere he could think of for the baby.

Joel tried to console a terrified Sarah. He wondered what should be done next. He glanced across the room and saw his favorite dog Callaban, stretched out on the floor in his characteristic manner. Front paws outstretched, eying the commotion. "My God," said Joel. "Is it possible…Callaban?" His voice trailed off. "No, it can't be." There was no sign of blood or any evidence to suggest that Callaban was the culprit or that he should be suspected of having anything to do with Baby Jen's disappearance.

Just then, a faint cry was heard. It came from the garbage bin. Joel dashed across the room and looked in. There was baby Jen wrapped in her blanket. She was warm and better still, she was alive. Joel picked her up and gave her to her mother. Sarah and Joel took turns holding her and hugging her. They kept repeating, "Oh, oh, sweet Jenny, little Jen, you are alive." They kissed her over and over again.

This sudden disappearance of baby Jenny from her crib had remained quite a mystery. No one knew for certain how the baby got there. However, Callaban was again scolded fiercely. He was reminded that he would pay dearly with his life, if he caused any harm to come to the baby.

One rather cold and bleak evening, as the setting sun emitted its last dying rays of sunlight, and the full moon was faintly visible in the sky; Joel and Sarah heard someone knocking furiously on their front door. Sarah answered it. She was nervously greeted by a youth, her neighbour's son, who lived some distance away. "Ms. Sarah," the youngster said breathlessly. "It's my mom. She is having the baby. She told me to let you know that it is due anytime now. Pa is in town and he is not expected until tomorrow. Please hurry, mom needs help now!"

Sarah wasted no time. She slipped on her shoes, tied a shawl around her neck, and put on a hat. She called out to Joel. "See you later hon, Mary needs me, her baby is due anytime now. I must hurry." "Be careful Sarah, hope all goes well." Joel replied. Sarah left in a hurry, with the neighbour's boy in tow.

Not very long after Sarah's departure, Joel went to visit his farm workers, who lived a very short distance away. They began a round of card games. He was so caught up in the games that time passed very quickly. Then, glancing at his watch, he said, "Sarah should be back by now. See you in the morning boys." He got up and left.

It was well past midnight. Sarah was hurrying home. As she approached the house, she noticed that it was in darkness. This seemed strange. 'Joel must be fast asleep,' she thought. Usually, he waited up for her. Then in the moonlight, she saw a figure emerging from the shadows. Her heart skipped a beat and she stood still. Before she could utter a word, Joel said, "I thought you would be home by now. My timing was right."

Joel never expected to hear what he heard next. "Joel, the baby, our baby Jen, where is she?" "Isn't she with you Sarah?" "No! I left her in her crib, knowing that you were at home." "But Sarah, I thought you took her along with you." "My God! Do you mean that our baby was alone by herself all this time!" blurted Joel. They both made a frantic dash to the door. There was no need to push it, because it was wide open. What they saw next made their hearts sink. Their worst fears were realized. They anxiously peered in the baby's crib. There was no sign of baby Jen. However, sitting at the foot of the crib was Callaban. He looked very tired. He was all covered with blood. In fact, there was blood everywhere.

Poor Sarah almost fainted, and slumped to the floor in one heap. Joel was shaking with rage. He lost total control of himself. "Callaban!" he shouted. "YOU DEVIL! How could you! Did I not tell you that I would kill you, if you ever did anything to my child? Now you leave me no choice."

Joel, in a fit of rage, rushed over and reached for his gun. He aimed it at Callaban's head. Callaban who was too weak to do anything, simply raised his head and looked at his master with mournful, blood-shot eyes as if to say, "Wait, I'm sorry old pal, but please don't shoot me. I have done nothing wrong."

As Joel was about to pull the trigger, Sarah involuntarily pushed his arm up. BANG! A shot rang out and grazed one of Callaban's ears. Callaban rolled over as though dead. The sudden impact jolted Sarah to full consciousness. It also brought a sharp baby's cry from an adjoining bedroom. Joel, still holding a smoking gun barrel in his hand, did not know whether he was dreaming. He hustled to the bedroom from which the cry came. There he saw baby Jenny covered with a blanket, alive and well.

At the foot of the bed, he saw a dead Timber wolf. His neck was broken. He was bleeding profusely. Joel soon realized that he had made a terrible mistake, almost a fatal one. He was full of remorse. He approached Callaban, put his hands around the wounded dog's neck and wept bitterly.

He kept repeating his dog's name, and all the while, sobbing like a baby, "Callaban, Callaban, poor Callaban, what have I done, what have I done, forgive me, forgive me?" Grief-stricken, he bowed his head and shook it sideways in utter despair. He was disgusted with himself. Sarah too, couldn't contain her grief. She sobbed like a child. They had both mistrusted and misjudged their favorite servant by making false assumptions ever since the arrival of Baby Jen.

Joel cleaned Callaban's wound, washed the blood from off his coat, gave him some warm soup and hugged him oh, so tenderly. "I should have thought clearly before acting. We should never have forgotten your kindness, faithfulness and loyalty. I am sorry for treating you that way old pal."

Callaban's faithfulness was rewarded almost with death from a rash judgment, and from a hasty and unfounded assumption. He had almost lost his life to preserve the life of another. Much like our Lord's, the only difference was that Jesus' life ended with death on the cross. He gave His life so we can be saved. Jesus did it out of love to save others, and what great love! So did Callaban!

Callaban was given a hero's reward. He became baby Jen's best friend and was allowed to play with her freely, whenever she wanted to play. Joel, on the other hand, had to live with the memory of his near fatal mistake, one which almost caused him to lose his most dependable, loyal, and faithful worker as well as his most trusted and best friend.

The Longest Story Ever Told

A very long time ago, in the kingdom of Zaphina lived wealthy and prosperous King Faz. He had an only daughter whose name was Princess Paulina. She was the most beautiful girl in all the land. Her hair was long, and black flowing gently on to her shoulders. Princess Paulina was very gracious in dealing with others. She was very loving, gentle and obedient, especially to her father whom she greatly admired and respected.

King Faz was an extremely jealous father and a very fussy old man. He seldom let the Princess out of his sight. In fact, she had very few friends, as he personally discouraged her from having any, for fear that she would love him less. In spite of his restrictions, however, Princess Paulina was particularly interested in a youth named Larry, whom she befriended at school. At the time, they were both students. They were being tutored, along with other children from the Royal household in a private school adjoining the Palace. Larry who was very kind-hearted, affectionate and charming, and whose parents worked for the king in his palace, had just turned seventeen. Princess Paulina was sixteen.

Because Larry was the son of one of the King's servants, Princess Paulina was never allowed to play or mix with him in the palace. King Faz didn't think that a commoner was fit company for his precious daughter. One day while at school, Paulina innocently confided in her cousin Maryanne about her attraction for Larry. Princess Paulina had always loved and treated Maryanne like a sister and trusted her completely.

Maryanne, however, had long envied Princess Paulina because of her charm and beauty. Now, Maryanne felt that she would be able to gain the king's favour if she disclosed to him what the Princess had told her. Accordingly, she secretly went to her uncle, King Faz and reported to him what the Princess had told her in confidence. King Faz, on learning about his daughter's affection for this young man, became instantly angry and enraged. He summoned Larry and his parents before his court and forthwith banished them from his Kingdom forever.

Larry and his parents moved to a neighboring country, where they lived a very simple but contented life. Many years went by, and during this time, there was no news of Larry and his parents. Meanwhile, Princess Paulina had reached the age when most young ladies got married, but this lovely

Princess was still single. King Faz' jealousy and fuss over his daughter had increased with age; and he rejected every one of her suitors. He found fault with them all. They were either too tall, too fat, too short, or too thin, while others were far too serious, or too funny for his liking. He used any and every excuse to discourage his daughter from getting seriously involved with anyone which could lead to her getting married. He did not want to lose her to anyone.

Becoming frustrated and tired of being alone for long periods of time, while all her relatives were getting married or engaged to be married, Princess Paulina approached her father in tears one day. "My dear father," she pleaded, " all my cousins are married. Soon I will be too old to get married and have children and you will have no grand children. Who will succeed you on the throne after you are gone? I would hate to reign by myself. Will you find me a husband?" King Faz was touched by his daughter's sincerity and her loyalty. "Yes, oh yes, I will, I will. This will give me great pleasure." He replied.

King Faz had a yearning for stories. He loved to hear stories being told. He spent all of his leisure hours listening to them. In fact, he had several storytellers in his employ in the palace. He spent days listening to stories and never got tired of them. He had an insatiable appetite for stories, and many times the stories would lull him to sleep. When he awoke from sleep, he would invite the storyteller to continue from where he had left off.

One day the King summoned all his chief advisors and court counselors to help advise him on how to find the best husband for his daughter. All their suggestions were rejected as worthless. He then had an idea, a brilliant one, as far as he was concerned. If he could find a man not much older than his daughter, one who could tell the longest story; this young man would have his daughter's hand in marriage. He felt that he himself would also be entertained by this storyteller.

Princess Paulina was somewhat distressed when she heard of his plan. However, she had no choice but to go along with it. In those days, children obeyed their parents without reservations and respected their opinions highly. It was considered terribly disrespectful if a son or daughter disobeyed his or her parents. In Princess Paulina's case, she had asked her father to find her a husband. She stood to lose everything and be disinherited, if she disobeyed him. Her fondest hope and desire were that her husband would be kind, handsome, caring and worthy of her love.

Notices were posted throughout and outside the kingdom for the young man who could tell the longest story. That man would get the Princess' hand in marriage. This decree was circulated far and wide. Every available bachelor, especially those who felt they had a long story came forward. The King had his secretaries record the length of time the stories took. Some stories were hours long. Others lasted for days. One went on as long as a week. Always King Faz would dismiss them with the promise that his secretary would get back to them. No decision would be made until all the interested suitors were heard.

Princess Paulina was becoming quite impatient. She couldn't understand what was the delay, unless she thought her father didn't really want her to get married. Several years had gone by and yet there was no result. "Could this be one of his tricks she wondered? How much longer must I wait?" She pondered to herself.

One day, a young but poor farmer was on his way to inform his aunt who lived in the kingdom of Zaphina about his parents' misfortune. His father and mother had both perished while trying to save a heifer that had fallen into a swift flowing stream. Unfortunately, they both drowned, and he was left to care to himself. Moreover, he intended to stay with his cousin during his visit while he sought work in order to feed and clothe himself.

This poor, young farmer learnt of the King's promise from his cousin. He felt that he had nothing to lose by accepting the king's invitation. Consequently, he borrowed and put on some of his cousin's clean clothes, and presented himself before the King. He was certain that he had a very long story to tell. King Faz looked at the young farmer disdainfully and said rather impatiently, "Now young man, I hope you are not here to waste my time. I've heard a story that lasted well over a month. Can you do better than that?" "I will try Sir, I will certainly try my best," said the young farmer nervously.

King Faz reluctantly summoned his secretary. He reclined on his throne and looked at the young man scornfully. He saw the callous hands of a farm labourer, and he became more outraged. In a gruff voice he said rather impatiently to the young farmer, "Well, what are you waiting on young man? Get on with it! Get on with it!" He then added in a stern voice. "I hope your story is going to be a really long one; or else you will pay dearly for wasting my time."

The young man was scared but he summoned enough courage and then began by saying: "Your Majesty King Faz, Sir, there once lived a farmer who owned thousands of acres of land. He planted the whole property with corn. The weather was ideal for the growing of corn; and the field yielded a rich harvest of yellow corn. Thousands of tons of corn grains were piled high as a mountain on the ground ready to be sold. Indeed, Your Majesty, there were so many grains of corn that it could cover a beach several hundred miles long.

Unfortunately, dear King, the owner of all this corn died. Having no relatives, this mountain of corn was left to stand in the open air. The corn became parched by the heat of the sun. Indeed the grains were so dry that water from the rain couldn't damage them." The young farmer went on. "Your Majesty, a severe drought overcame the land not too long after. It wiped out every living thing for miles around. However, there survived one insect and its family. This insect was a mother locust. She too had lost her mate who had fed his children everything he could find and even went hungry himself, for days until he eventually died of hunger."

King Faz shifted uneasily in his chair. He asked for a drink, gobbled it up in gulps, then reclined on his throne and waved his right hand impatiently at the young man saying, "Get on with it, get on with it!" The young man continued, "Your Majesty, Sir, the mother locust loved her family dearly, and she was determined to feed her children. She was now tired and weak after several days of searching for food to feed her dear little ones. Indeed, she had flown just about everywhere to see whether she could find even a morsel of food for her starving, hungry children, who were relying on her help to keep them alive. Then, she came upon a mountain, which seemed to rise from the middle of a plain. Being tired from flying around for such a long time, she decided to rest there to regain her failing strength so that she could continue her search."

"Your Majesty, there was not a tree nor a blade of grass on this mountain, which seemed to be covered with a multitude of yellow and brown pebbles. Being very hungry, she bit into one of the pebbles and to her amazement, she discovered that this mountain was in fact stacked grains of corn. Though very tired, mother locust became very excited and happy. She was beside herself with joy." "Oh, if only I could carry some of these grains of corn to my family, we would never go hungry again." She said to herself.

"But Your Majesty, mama locust had a major problem. She lived quite a distance away from the newly found supply of food, and her children were far too young and weak to fly. Therefore, since they could not get to the mountain of corn to feed, she was determined to take the corn to them. Now, she could think of only one way to carry all this food. She had no other means but to carry it one grain at a time. Thus, this dutiful mama locust thinking only of the welfare of her family set about her task dutifully, so her dear little ones would never go hungry again."

"Mama locust gleefully took one grain of corn flew the whole distance to her home and fed one of her starving babies. She flew back to the huge mountain of corn took another grain and returned home to feed another one of her hungry children." The young farmer took a sip of water and continued. "Mama locust went for another grain of corn, carried it to her home and fed another one of her weak children. Again, and again, mama locust returned to the mound, and took yet another grain of corn to her home. Her family ate it all up but they were still very hungry, not having

eaten for several days before. So away mama locust went and fetched another grain of corn and took it to her home."

The young man went on, "What a dutiful and diligent worker was this mother locust! Your Majesty, Sir, she intended to carry all this corn to her family, so no famine would ever affect them again. She never missed one minute's work. Mama locust came, took another grain of corn and flew away. Again, she came to the mound of corn, took another grain and flew away." The young farmer kept repeating this, time and time again.

The young farmer said to the king, "King Faz, Sir, after several months the locust was able to carry off only a very, very tiny portion of that mountainous pile of corn. The bulk of corn still lay in a huge mound in the same place. Your Majesty, Sir, mama locust came to the mound of corn, took one grain and flew away. She came back, took yet another grain and flew away. She came again, took another grain, flew away, and fed her family." The king was becoming very impatient; as days gave way to weeks, and weeks into months, and months into years. "Yet, this diligent worker, Mama locust never got tired of providing for her family. She just kept going back for more corn and she would remove just one grain at a time, because that was all she was capable of carrying at a time."

King Faz who was now very old, thought to himself, "My dear daughter would be old indeed, and past child-bearing age by the time that this silly locust and his family would have exhausted all those grains of corn. That one locust could never transport all that corn in my life-time." In desperation, he asked the young farmer. "Young man, when do you expect your silly locust to transport that huge supply of corn to her home and family?" "Perhaps for decades, my Lord," came the reply. "Is that so, young man?" "Yes, Your Majesty, mama locust was too kind to neglect her family. Remember now, she could take only one grain at a time." "Didn't her family ever grow up to help her?" the King asked angrily. "Yes, Your Majesty, but they had grown too fat with the corn and so they could not fly." Confused and not wanting to go back on his promise, King Faz impatiently sent for his daughter. He was certain that she would never choose a farmer's boy.

Princess Paulina reluctantly entered the palace with downcast eyes and stood before the throne where her father sat. Her maid had told her that the man whom her father had chosen for her, and to whom she was about to wed, was no other than a poor, wretched farmer's boy. His only claim to fame was that ridiculous story of the locust. The Princess was distraught and very sad indeed. "How could my dad do this to me?" She mused. "Princess Paulina!" the King said in a rather gruff, disappointing and disgusting tone of voice, "here's your future husband. You can have him if you want, but...," He stopped short, hoping that she would refuse this offer of a husband.

Princess Paulina who had a heart of gold was far too kind and gentle to embarrass this poor, young farmer, so she raised her eyes timidly to look at him and to tell him that she was not yet prepared for marriage. As their eyes met, however, she instantly recognized the gleam in his eyes, his curly black hair, and the dimple on his chin. Speechlessly, they gazed into each other's eyes. "Oh Larry, my dear Larry, thank God it's you! You're safe. Oh, how have I missed you!" "Paulina, my dear, dear Paulina, I have never forgotten you. Never did I dream that I would ever see you again." They wept tears of joy as they locked in a tight embrace.

King Faz did not know what to make of this. He stared in disbelief. What choice did he have but to accept this young man, and to give his daughter's hand in marriage. He had given his word and had to live by it. Later that very day, wedding bells chimed in a most beautiful nuptial ceremony the palace had ever witnessed. Larry and princess Paulina waltzed to the strains of Johann Strauss' Voices of Spring, and left to honeymoon on an Emerald Island. They invited Larry's cousin, and his aunt to live in the palace with them.

What a wonderful, loving and gracious couple were Larry and Paulina, the fairest the land of Zaphina had ever seen! As for King Faz, he gave them his blessing, and lived for many years, but he never wanted to hear another story again. For in his sleep and in his dreams, he could still see the dutiful mama locust returning time and time again, to remove just one grain of corn at a time from that mountainous pile, to feed her dear little ones.

END OF AN ERA

He was reputed to be one of the world's greatest boxers of all times. He was cunning, cagey and crafty. In his prime, his opponents seldom ever went the final round. He moved around the ring with such agility and nimbleness, that his foes had the greatest difficulty in keeping up with him. His business-like approach, coupled with his artistic flair made him an instant favorite with the boxing fans. Combatants' knees buckled and they fell like lame ducks under his persistent jabbing intermingled with ferocious pummeling.

He had a lean muscular body, which glistened as he worked himself into a sweat. Broad-chested, square-shouldered and tall, he cut an imposing figure. He would skip and dance around the ring like a ballerina using the ropes to its fullest advantage. Moving rhythmically, he would punch and jab his opponents. Then with a flurry of uppercuts executed with lightening speed, he would dish out the most punishing blows on his opponents.

Fighter after fighter yielded to this onslaught and his evasive but aggressive style. Most of the time, he escaped unscathed. His handsome features showed little evidence of fatigue or battering, except for the sweat that oozed from every pore in his lithe body when he fought or trained.

But now, Tommy was forty-five. He bulged in the middle. His steps had slowed to a somewhat 'drag and halt' in the ring. Now he was prone to lounge forward rather often, and even awkwardly. Sometimes he stumbled as he attempted desperately to hit his target. He no longer looked the prize-fighter, the champion that he once was.

Tonight, standing in the ring acknowledging the applause of the fans, he cut a rather pathetic figure, very unlike the imposing stalwart that he used to be. He looked somewhat obese. Yet, he was determined to prove that he was one of the greatest fighters in his century. He felt within himself that he could win this fight. There was a look of defiance in his eyes, the glow of that fighting spirit, which seems to characterize all great fighters.

His opponent, a young and energetic boxer seemed anxious to begin the fight. Maddox, the challenger was a muscular, rugged individual. His well-built frame was supported by bulging thighs. He had huge arms and a broad chest. He was a relatively new -comer to the ring, but he had a few victories under his belt, and he had also won his bouts convincingly.

There was that feeling of expectancy mixed with pathos in the air. Some fans felt that Tommy, who for many years was their favorite champion, had no business being in the ring so late in his career. Others felt that because of his wealth of experience, he deserved this chance. In any event, he had a great deal of support from a large group of faithful supporters. After all, he had been the champ for many years, and he had successfully defended his title on many occasions. He was certainly a skilled boxer. He knew how to make effective use of the ropes. He could throw devastating punches, and he knew how to evade those of his opponents.

Yet, one couldn't help but sense his feeling of uncertainty. And in the arena that night, there seemed to be an uneasy tenseness in the atmosphere, which tended to linger like mist on a foggy day. Among the boxing fans, there was a feeling of apprehension, which can best be described as one of impending doom.

Tommy with his trainer by his side entered the ring to tumultuous greetings from his fans. He was still their favorite despite his age. He clowned around the ring as though he had everything under control. He acknowledged their support by blowing kisses to them. There were some tame boos but these faded into the background. He was closely followed into the ring by Maddox, who also had his supporters but they were fewer in number. There were hisses, wild cheering and some boos as well, as he too entered the ring.

The ring announcer positioned himself in the center of the ring, and with a commanding voice, which reached a crescendo then trailed off, he introduced each fighter to the audience. "In the right corner from Miami, weighing 220 pounds, and sporting blue shorts, the challenger, the young and dangerous Ma....ddox! In the left corner, from Texas, weighing 268 pounds and wearing red shorts, the former heavyweight champion of the world, To...mmy Harris! Your referee for tonight's bout is Libby Long."

The referee then brought the two boxers to the center of the ring, where they stood toe to toe, eyeballing each other with unblinking stares. Each tried to psyche out the other. This is a familiar tactic commonly used by most boxers. The referee gave his final instructions to the boxers and asked them to keep the fight clean, and to avoid low blows. The bell sounded and the fight was now underway.

Maddox moved cagily. He danced about nimbly on his toes looking rather business-like. Tommy plodded along flat-footed. He moved rather clumsily. This prompted the fight commentator to remark that he was now only a shadow of his former self. He was so slow that he had difficulty keeping up with the quicker, and more youthful and energetic Maddox. The first round concluded without much damage to either boxer.

In the opening of the second round, Tommy repeatedly missed his target. Occasionally, he landed a blow, but this was countered with left and right combinations to his body by his opponent. Suddenly there was an uproar from the crowd as Tommy landed one of his rare punches that grazed Maddox's forehead. No sooner did this happen, it was countered by a ferocious uppercut that jolted Tommy's head backward. Fortunately, he was able to hang on and was saved by the bell. Round two had come to an end.

The following rounds were disheartening for Tommy's fans to witness. Repeatedly he was short of his mark with his punches, which were often wild. He seemed to be looking for just that one big punch which would end the fight. On the other hand, Maddox was putting on a show. He targeted his opponent with left-right combinations, which seemed to hurt the much older man when they landed as they often did.

Tommy was noted for his big heart. He was a courageous fighter. He wasn't the type of fighter to throw in the towel without putting forth his best effort. Indeed, it couldn't be said that he wasn't trying his best. Age had slowed him down terribly, but he could still take a punch and dish one out when given the chance. Tonight however, he had absorbed much punishment from the youthful Maddox. He seemed tired and was unable to escape the battering. He just stood there, occasionally and instinctively sticking out his hand to jab Maddox, or to deflect some of Maddox's blows. However, his offensive and defensive tactics had little or no effect on the aggressiveness and confidence of the youthful Maddox.

The pounding continued round after round. The crowd grew deadly silent. There were loud groans as blow after blow landed in quick succession on the almost defenseless Tommy. The fans felt his hurt. His face was puffy, his eyes were half-shut, and blood oozed from his nostrils and mouth. Round five was over. Tommy hobbled or rather staggered to his corner in a daze from the beating.

His trainer gave him his water bottle, mopped the sweat and blood from off his brow and face with a wet sponge. His doctor worked on the cut over his right eye, and desperately tried to stop the flow of blood from his nostrils and mouth. The bleeding stopped temporarily. Tommy looked somewhat bewildered. Most of the fans felt that he should continue no longer and should concede the fight, but almost miraculously, he answered the bell to begin the sixth round.

Fighting Maddox darted from his corner as a hungry tiger going after its kill. Tommy groggily ambled forward on unsteady legs to meet Maddox at the center of the ring. They squared off, and again the pounding continued. Time and time again, Tommy swung but his punches missed their target. While Maddox's left-right combinations beat a steady rhythm on Tommy's body. The wonder of it all was that gallant Tommy was still on his feet.

Tommy was fighting instinctively, and wondered whether he could strike it lucky. He was hoping to land just that one lucky punch. "May-be, I can pull it off," he thought to himself. Unfortunately, this did not happen, as his punches lacked power, and he had weakened considerably from the vicious punishment that he had absorbed. He was being constantly hit like a punching bag. “Rat-tap-tap,” came the blows in rapid succession. At one point, he stumbled and was rocked backward with the force of Maddox’s power punches. He winced, but he did not fall.

Everyone in the stadium, including Maddox’s fans felt sorry for this once proud and gallant boxer. Today he had moved rather clumsily in the ring and now stood in a daze after the pummeling he had absorbed. How the mighty has fallen! His time had come. This was the moment. Tommy was badly beaten up. Out-punched, out-boxed, and out-maneuvered. He cut a sad figure indeed in the ring. Being unable to defend himself, the referee had no other recourse but to stop the fight and raise Maddox's hand in victory. Maddox won a decisive victory by TKO (Technical Knockout).

Tommy now totally battered, lowered his head dejectedly. He was a beaten man. Blood flowed from his nostrils, from cuts over his eyes, and from a foaming mouth. The crowd filed out of the stadium in stunned silence. They had just witnessed the end of an era.

One fan was heard saying, "At forty-five, why did Tommy go into the ring, and what was he trying to prove?" "Well, I guess he felt history might repeat itself," said another. "Yes, but not tonight…!" interrupted a third. "Good grief, what a licking he absorbed," they all chimed in.

His son Tommy Junior, who was sitting at ringside, felt sadness for his dad. He knew that his dad was a proud man. He thought he had heard his father say, "I want a rematch." He knew he had to do something before it was too late. Tommy was led through a maze of people to his dressing room. Junior followed his dad closely into the dressing room.

In the dressing room, Junior went up to his dad, and hugged him ever so tightly and kissed him. "Dad," he said, "You're still the greatest. You're still my number one hero." His dad looked at him through blood-shot eyes, not knowing what to say. Junior continued. "Dad you've always told me to listen when others speak. Now, please listen to me. Remember when I played too rough with my sister. You said, Knock it off Junior. You should know when to stop. You were right dad. You said to me, Quit it before somebody gets hurt! I did as you said dad and I was glad that I did. I took your advice. Now Dad, I think you ought to know when to quit too. You are not as young as you used to be, and though you are still a classy boxer, you have past your prime. There is nothing more for you to prove Dad. The

next time you might not be as lucky. Do you recall the song popularized by Brook Benton. The lyrics went like this dad. ‘If Mother Nature doesn't get you, Father time sure will.’ Dad, Brook Benton knew what he was singing about. It’s time to give up boxing. Please Dad!” Junior pleaded.

Tommy looked at his son as tears streamed from puffy eyes. He knew Junior was right, but he had allowed pride to stand in his way. He had taken a good pounding from a much younger, stronger, and faster opponent. There was nothing really to be ashamed of. He reached over to Junior and said, “Come here Son, I love you, ...and thank you Junior.” They locked in a tight embrace, father and son. And after a drawn-out silence, Tommy said, “I promise that l will never get back in the ring again. I guess there is no fool like an old fool.”

Five Wishes

In the far north in the kingdom of Zanora, and hundreds of miles from any large urban centre lived an old couple, Marlin and Tara, in an old run-down shack. Times were hard and jobs were almost non- existent because of a growing recession. Their only means of livelihood came from fishing.

Marlin was an expert fisherman, and his fishing skills, which he had acquired when he was a boy, enabled him to put food quite regularly on the table. His wife Tara was a wonderful cook. She would take great delight in preparing the catch of the day, which Marlin brought home almost on a daily basis. Tara's meals were tasty, and it was interesting to see how she was able to make do with the little food that they had in the house.

However, a few days had gone by and poor Marlin's fishing luck had taken a turn for the worse. During this period after many tireless hours spent fishing off the seashore, he would return home empty handed. Each day Tara would wait and watch eagerly for his return, and when he opened the front door to let himself in, she would greet him with a wry smile saying, "Hi Marlin, any luck today?" To which he would reply rather sullenly, "Sorry Ta, dear, I didn't get as much as a nibble today."

This unfortunate turn of events continued for several days longer, and with each passing day, Tara became increasingly anxious and impatient. What little food they had in the house was soon exhausted and there was very little left for them to eat. To make matters worse, whenever Marlin came home with no catch after the day's fishing, Tara no longer greeted him with her usual smile, instead she would chide, insult and reproach him, saying, "See Marlin, we should never have come to live here in the first place. I always had my doubts about living in this remote place. I hate it here."

In reply, Marlin would try to remind her of the series of unfortunate circumstances in their lives that had brought about their present situation. Both Tara and Marlin's parents had lost their lives on a hunting trip when Tara and Marlin were still young. As a result, they had no one on whom to depend for assistance. Not long after their parents' death, they got married and started a small farming business, which provided them with enough resources on which to live. Unfortunately, after a few successive harvests, they experienced a severe drought which caused immeasurable damage to their crops, and they had to take out a bank loan to help maintain the farm.

Worst yet, late in the following season, severe rainstorms and a tornado completely destroyed everything on the farm. Since they had no insurance on the farm, and no means of repaying the bank loan, the bank stepped in and repossessed the farm and what little remaining equipment they had to work the farm. This catastrophe was soon followed by a countrywide lingering recession, and Tara and Marlin could find no work to support themselves.

Marlin was too proud and independent a man to go on welfare, so he and Tara agreed to move to this remote area, where he was sure they could survive and make a living off fishing. Now another day had gone by and they both began to feel the pangs of hunger. Marlin too was beginning to experience a sense of guilt. 'Today,' he thought to himself, 'I must catch something, I am determined to bring home food.'

The morning was cold and bleak. It was early dawn and darkness still hung in the air when Marlin set out from his home. The bitingly cold wind howled in the trees, and the leaves trembled as though in fright. Poor Marlin, wearing a heavy coat buttoned up to his neck, with his rod and other fishing gear in hand, strolled along a narrow path that led to the sea. He was cold and hungry but he was determined to make a catch. 'Today, I must succeed,' he kept repeating to himself.

On arriving on the seashore, Marlin wasted no time. He placed his fishing gear on a huge rock near the water, baited his hook and cast it far into the sea. The line with the baited hook fluttered briefly in the breeze, then the hook anchored by a lead weight, sank and disappeared into the choppy waters.

Marlin teasingly and skillfully played the hook, hoping to lure any fish that chanced to swim by to take the bait, but nothing happened. With the same determination and ultimate patience, which tend to characterize a good fisherman, Marlin, using a different bait each time, cast his hook again and again into the sea.

Eventually, and not until late afternoon that Marlin had a strong hit as a fish took the bait. With the skill of an experienced fisherman, he set his hook. There was a strong tug on the line as the fish tried to escape from the baited hook. From the strong pull on the line, Marlin could feel the weight of the fish. "This one is a really big one, I can't allow him to get away," he said to himself. His heart pounded fiercely in his chest. "Oh, how happy Tara will be! Food, glorious food!" For indeed he did care a great deal for Tara, and he too was a very hungry man.

Time and time again, his line would alternately stiffen then go slack as the struggling fish tried to dislodge the hook in its mouth. At such times,
when the line became taut, he would give the line some slack, and then he would gradually reel it in. On one occasion, the fish made an arc in the air as it jumped out of the water. This fish was indeed a big one! Marlin continued to play the fish with all the expertise he had acquired over the years as a fisherman, and lucky for him, he was a very strong man. The fish fought Marlin for well over half- an- hour and as it began to tire, Marlin reeled in all of his strong nylon line and at last landed the 'monster fish.'

For the very first time in his life as a fisherman, Marlin was nervous. He had caught many fishes in the past, and some were as large as this one, but there was something different about this fish. It was the most unusual looking fish he had ever seen. Sure enough, it had a streamlined body, but its tail, fins, gills and scales shone like polished gold even in the fading light.

Marlin had never caught a fish as beautiful as this one, so he held it in both hands to take a closer look at it and admire it. For a brief moment, the fish opened its eyes. There was a distinctive human-like quality about it, and though Marlin was really hungry, the thought of frying this one repulsed him; but then, he thought of Tara, and wondered, how happy she would be to feast on this big one with much or it left over for several days.

He was just about to bag the fish to take it home when it happened. To his utter amazement, the fish opened its mouth and began to speak. "Kind Sir," it said. "My name is Prince Bonito, once a handsome young man, I shared the palace with my father King Olaf and my mother, Queen Leita. I behaved badly, often disobeyed my parents and ran away from home on numerous occasions when they threatened to punish me."

He continued, "I befriended an old magician who promised to help cure me of my wicked ways. Accordingly, he took me to a witch who cast a spell on me and turned me into a fish. The witch said that my spell would be broken and I would return to my former self, only if I performed some good deeds. She gave me five wishes to use." "Good Sir, if you would release me I would grant you the five wishes the witch gave me. You can request anything and it will be done; the witch's spell would be broken, and I would be free to return to my parents' palace."

Marlin listened with keen interest. He became dumbfounded, and knew not what to make of this proposition. He hesitated before making up his mind as to whether he should accept this offer. Then the fish added: "You are Marlin, aren't you?" I remember when you lost your farm in the great depression. Now if you spare my life, you can have the five wishes. You will be able to make your wife, Tara very happy. The only condition for your wife's happiness and yours is that you must not exceed the five wishes. Please release me Sir, and you would never regret it."

Marlin looked long and hard at the fish. He thought how happy he could make Tara, so he kept repeating to himself: 'Five wishes!' In any case, it didn't seem right to kill a 'prince- turned- fish,' and especially a prince who knew him personally.

Then Marlin said, "Prince Bonito, I will spare your life but don't forget your promises." "Indeed not, Good Sir," replied the fish. Marlin looked at the lovely, big, blue eyes of the fish and his kind heart melted within him. He released the fish. There was a great splash in the water, and Marlin followed it with his eyes, then turned and left for home; and you can easily imagine how anxious he was to get home. 'Wait till I tell Tara,' he said to himself. 'She will be ecstatic!'

Meanwhile Tara was eagerly but patiently awaiting Marlin's return. When she saw Marlin approaching empty-handed, she became bitterly disappointed. Yet, there was something strange about him that she couldn't understand. Whenever he caught nothing, he usually walked very slowly with downcast eyes, but now he was walking briskly with upraised head. She was truly baffled by his demeanour.

As he got within an earshot of her, she said to him, "Where is it Marlin? Where is it?" "Where is what Tara?" replied Marlin. "The fish Marlin, the fish!" "Oh, dear I let him go," said Marlin. "What! Uttered Tara in disbelief, here I am hungry and starving and all you can say is that you let him go," "Are you crazy old man!" Tara added indignantly. "You must be losing it." She added. "Hear me out, please Tara, hear me out. Will you?" Marlin responded.

“NO, I won’t hear you out! I’m sick and tired of your excuses Marlin, tired and sick! Do you hear me?” shouted Tara. To which Marlin responded calmly, “Are you finished ranting Tara? Now, would you please listen to me?” Tara was taken back by his quiet calmness. She pretended that she did not care to listen to him, but secretly she was anxious to hear what he had to say.

“Tara, I had a most unusual experience today. See, Tara, I did catch a fish, but he was astonishingly beautiful and he talked.” said Marlin. Tara interrupted, “What!” She exploded, “Are you nuts! A talking fish, well what’s next?” Marlin lowered his head and in a calm voice continued, “Do you remember King Olaf and his wayward son Prince Bonito, who ran away from the palace. Well, a witch cast a spell on him and turned him into a fish. I caught him, and because I spared his life he promised me five wishes.” Imagine Tara, we can wish for anything and our wishes would be granted; just think about it Tara, anything at all.”

“Well Marlin what are you waiting on? Go to the fish now and tell him that your wife is very hungry and we have nothing in the house to eat. Marlin wasted no time. He hurried to the very spot near the sea where he had released the fish, perched himself atop a rock and shouted out: “O Prince of the sea, please listen to me, my wife is very hungry and she would like to have some food.” Instantly there was a giant splash, and Prince Bonito, the fish, surfaced from the water and said, “Go home Marlin, it’s already there.”

Marlin left for his home at a very brisk pace. On the way home, he was a bit troubled and wondered whether he was the fool that Tara thought him to be. When he arrived at his home however, he just couldn’t believe his eyes. There was the widest assortment of foods he had ever seen, roast beef, lamb chops, fried chicken, salads, potatoes and vegetables. His old kitchen cupboards were stocked with food that could last for several months. Tara was gushing with joy as she welcomed Marlin home and they ate to their heart’s content.

Then Tara, her eyes all lit up now turned to her husband and said, “Now Marlin, go back to that golden fish and tell him that your wife needs a bigger house to live in.” So, Marlin set off once more. He completed the two-mile journey in record time. It was late evening when he reached the sea shore, and again standing on top of the rock, he repeated the same words: “Oh Prince of the sea listen to me, my wife is unhappy in our little house, she wants a much bigger one.” There was a moment’s hesitation, then the fish,

Prince Bonito stood on his tail and said, "Marlin, your wish is granted, go home, it's already there."

Marlin trotted home as fast as his legs would carry him, but being a bit weak from his recent ordeals, the journey took him a bit longer. On reaching home, Marlin was so surprised with what he saw that he almost collapsed from a shortness of breadth. For in place of their once run-down shack, there now stood a gorgeous mansion.

Inside the mansion, chandeliers hung from the ceiling, while luxurious furniture with velvet cushions adorned the living room. Each of the seven bedrooms had gold canopy beds covered with exquisitely embroidered sheets; and one-of-a-kind lounging chairs bedecked an open patio.

Marlin could never have imagined anything as beautiful as that mansion. "Tara," he said, "what a magnificent home!" "Indeed, Marlin, indeed! But, I can't take care of this big house all by myself,' she said, "Go to the Fish again and tell him that your wife is not happy as she will have to do much work taking care of such a big house. Tell him that I need maids, servants and butlers to help me."

Tara carried away by all that material wealth, never stopped to consider how many wishes she had already used up. She had requested food, a new home, servants which included butlers and maids. With a wave of her hand, she dismissed Marlin.

Of course, Marlin would do anything to please his wife, and after all, the Prince- turned- fish had promised him five wishes. Without any hesitation Marlin said, "OK, Tara, I'm on my way." He set off on foot again and soon arrived on the beach.

It was now late at night, but the half-moon in the sky gave sufficient light, so Marlin could see the water in the sea clearly. He perched himself on the familiar rock, and with confidence repeated the now famous words: "Oh Prince of the sea, listen to me, my wife is still unhappy because she needs maids, butlers and servants; and she also needs lots of new clothes."

Prince Bonito with a giant splash emerged from the sea. He seemed a little annoyed, but he would keep his promise. He stood on his golden tail as before and spouting some water said, "Marlin go home, your wishes are granted."

Without much ado, Marlin retraced his steps, and got home in record time, but unlike the other times, there was no need to open the doors. Indeed there

was a butler opening the door to let him in. There were servants everywhere, and maids were waiting on Tara. Marlin saw her dressed in a long flowing gown with matching jewellery. Her closets and dresser were filled with the finest garments.

Tara kept admiring herself in the mirror and called on her maids to attend to her every need. Marlin looked at his wife adoringly. "My dear Tara," he said, "You certainly look very beautiful." "Yes, I agree," replied Tara, "but

Marlin, to make my happiness complete, I wish to be a queen. True, I do have maids, servants and butlers at my disposal, but I need a crown. Just think of it Marlin, having all the prestige that goes with being a queen."

Marlin looked at his wife in disbelief. Tara, however, took little notice of him. She simply said, "Marlin, go to Prince Bonito and let him know how sad I am, tell him that I want to be a queen." Marlin said, "But, Tara, do you think that I should disturb the Prince again?" "Well Marlin," she retorted, "must I remind you that you saved his life. He gave you five wishes, didn't he? Just think Marlin, as a queen I would have power to do as I please. We would never go hungry again. Now go Marlin, I am waiting."

Marlin left home rather reluctantly, for he was tired and hated to disturb Prince Bonito who had so far lived up to his promises. In addition, it was past midnight and he felt that Prince Bonito would be sound asleep, but then he didn't want to displease his dear wife. And though the journey took a little longer time to complete, he was soon standing on the same rock, and again addressed the fish in the following words: "Oh Prince of the sea, please listen to me, my wife is sad." Before uttering another word, Prince Bonito said in a disturbing voice. "Now Marlin, what is it?" "It's my wife, she wants to be a queen." Said Marlin."

"A queen she would be," said Prince Bonito. "Go home it's already done," and he disappeared beneath the waves. Marlin once more returned home by the same route he had journeyed so many times before. When he went inside his house, he found Tara seated on an elaborate throne; and on her head she wore a golden crown studded with diamonds. She looked resplendent in the light.

Marlin, feeling proud of his wife Her Majesty Queen Tara, came and stood close to her to admire her in all her splendour. However, Tara taking one quick glance at Marlin said in a distasteful tone of voice. "Marlin, have you looked at your self lately? You look so ordinary, I don't think that I would ever be happy to live with you the way you are. A queen needs a king, go this minute to the Prince and tell him that your wife is very unhappy, and that she needs a king and that king must be you, Marlin."

Marlin stood puzzled, hurt and humiliated. He certainly did not want to disturb Prince Bonito yet another time, but he also did not want to lose Tara. Furthermore, he had lost count of the number of wishes that the Prince had fulfilled. He also reasoned that being king, he would never have to work hard again for the rest of his life, and that he would have everything.

So Marlin, tired from a lack of sleep, set out for the sea yet once more to make his request. The early morning air was cold and nippy. Dark, heavy clouds were everywhere in the sky. The chilling winds caused him to hug himself tightly as he tried to walk briskly to keep himself warm. Coming to the edge of the sea, he climbed the fateful rock to summon the Prince.

The sea was foaming, and the waters of the sea choppy. High billowy waves piled one on top of the other and crashed ashore spraying everything in it's way. Poor Marlin, shivering from the cold winds gusting from off the sea chanted the same refrain in as loud a voice as he could muster, "O, Prince of the sea, please listen to me. My wife is very sad and unhappy. She needs a king to live with and she wants me to be that king."

The angry waters became angrier. A streak of lightening lit up the dark sky, and thunder roared menacingly in the vast emptiness of space. Then came a gigantic splash, as Prince Bonito balancing himself on his tail on the crest of a huge wave greeted Marlin in a tremulous voice. "What now Marlin! What is it you want?" "O, Prince, it's my wife, she wants me to be a king." Prince Bonito became very sad, as tears streamed from his eyes, and he said to Marlin, "how many wishes did I offer you?" "I think five, O, Prince," said Marlin. "And how many have you already received?" asked the Prince. Marlin thought for a while, but he could not remember. He was so completely carried away and overwhelmed by the events of the day, that he seemed to have lost count and was totally confused.

Prince Bonito using his golden fins continued to balance himself on his tail, and said to Marlin, "You have exceeded your fifth wish. Do you remember my telling you that you should never exceed five wishes? Do you understand what you have done?" "I'm very sorry Prince," said the apologetic Marlin. "I too, am very sorry Marlin, said the Prince-turned-fish. I would have hoped that things would have ended differently." Having said this Prince Bonito dived under the water and disappeared from sight.

He left Marlin standing there shivering in the coldness holding his old fisherman's rod, and wearing his old worn out pants and a ragged shirt, over which he wore an old weather beaten overcoat.

A moment later, Prince Bonito reappeared and said to Marlin, "Now Marlin, go to Tara your wife and let her know what her greed has caused. And Marlin, be strong! Let your lesson be a lesson to all. Goodbye, my friend."

With another giant splash, Prince Bonito disappeared from sight into the sea. Marlin returned home to his former old and dilapidated shack. Tara looked haggard and hungry in her tattered clothes. There was no need for words. They both cried upon each other's shoulder, and for once, each realized how important it is to make the best of what one has.

Two months later, there was a knock on the door of their shack. Prince Bonito had never forgotten Marlin's kindness in sparing his life after being caught as a fish. He realized that one kind deed deserves another, so he had dispatched two of his guards to rescue Marlin and Tara from a life of poverty. Marlin and Tara however sent words of thanks to the Prince via the guards, having decided to stay where they were and make the best of what little they had.

THE GREAT DEBATE

At a world-wide conference of edible fruit-bearing trees, plants, shrubs and vines, a heated argument arose as to which of them produced the fruit most highly favoured by human beings. After several minutes of verbal wrangling that proved fruitless, to use a pun, they agreed to participate in an orderly, structured debate. The purpose of this verbal exercise was to determine which of them could lay claim legitimately, to producing the fruit most favoured by humankind.

One female plant representing each species would participate in the debate since only they had the honour of producing the fruits. Their male counterparts would have the unenviable tasks of being impartial judges and objective observers, even though some of them may have helped in the production of the fruits in question.

It was further suggested that in the interest of a more equitable, agreeable, and just decision of the final outcome of the debate, all the edible fruits and food producing plant species would be classified according to the environment in which they live, their natural habitat. Accordingly, two major groups were identified and classified as Group A and Group B respectively. Group A would represent all plant species that grow in temperate regions; and group B would represent all those that are native to tropical regions.

It was further agreed that in order to eliminate any bias or prejudice, and to ensure that the most objective approach be taken in the judging of this Great Debate, a few chosen trees were awarded the unenviable distinction of officiating as judicial advisors to the judges-in-chief.

In temperate regions, the Douglas Fir, the Balsam Pine and the Mighty Oak were chosen to serve as judicial advisors. For the tropical regions, the Immortelle tree, the Mahogany and the Cedar were the judicial advisors selected. The Balata, a huge tree, native to the tropics was considered, but was ruled ineligible, because it was classified as a female plant as she did produce a small but delicious fruit and could therefore participate and compete in the debate as a contestant.

Two judges-in-chief were selected, one for each of the two regions. In matters of dispute or disagreement, the judge-in-chief's decision was final. There would be no recourse to any other authority.

Mr. Lichen, a rather inconspicuous plant and a native species of the tundra region, was chosen judge-in-chief for the contestants in temperate regions. It was felt that his ability to thrive successfully in the harshest environment, in the cold, bleak tundra regions, where no other plant thrives comfortably, except for some mosses, gave him the character, durability and strength that would be required to adjudicate the debate successfully.

The choice for judge-in-chief to represent plants in tropical region fell to one, Mr. Cactus, whom everyone thought deserved this distinction, as he was able to withstand the most severe drought conditions, typically of his home, the hot, sandy, desert waste lands in that region. There was an objection from the Date Palm, which claimed that some species of Cacti do produce fruits and could be classified as female plants. Miss Date Palm also claimed that she too lived in hot desert conditions and should be considered for the post. She was ruled out of order, however, on the grounds that not only did she produce a sweet, delicious fruit, but also thrived best in an oasis, and was not a hardy survivor like this Mr. Cactus, who was indeed a male plant.

Several judging criteria were identified as the basis for declaring the winner of each of the two groups. Points would be given to the contestant who could demonstrate very clearly, her overall importance to the welfare of human beings. Once the two winners were identified for Group A and B, these two ladies would then go head-to-head in a final debate to determine the overall champion fruit and be crowned queen of all the plant species.

Now, the Great Debate was about to begin. Mr. Lichen and Mr. Cactus took their respective places at the head of the judges' table along with the judicial advisors seated at adjoining tables. Just before the judges brought the proceedings to order to begin the debate, a side bar argument arose among the astonishingly large number of fruits and food producing plants. The judges decided that they would allow these plants a little time to blow off steam, as it would then be easier to control the debate.

Miss Cocochat, a tiny berry that grows on an uncultivated vine in the tropics started to argue. She is so tiny that she can be seen with the naked eye, only with the greatest difficulty. In her shrill voice she was heard to say, "If there's such a thing as evolution of species, why have I remained so small and inconspicuous all these years, so that only a very few people ever see me, and fewer still have ever tasted my juice. Don't you think I would have loved to become a fruit tree that bears such a delightful fruit as Miss Sugar Apple? She has a relatively large and clearly visible body. She is so delicious, pulpy, and sweet to the taste. Everyone fusses over her, but here I am a puny nonentity."

"Yea," chimed in Miss Banana who added in a sarcastic tone of voice, "It is true that I can be eaten green when cooked, or be eaten as I am, when ripe, or be made into a banana punch or a banana ice cream split. I can be fried, pounded and made into banana cake and bread, but my brothers, sisters and I are forever clustered in bunches. I have no individuality and no privacy. Worse yet, my jacket can split open by itself when I am fully ripe exposing my naked body. Don't you think that I would have much preferred to have a single stem all to myself like a guava or a pomme de rac, and can dangle to tempt those school girls and boys?"

"How ungrateful of you, Miss Banana! Almost every one on earth loves you. Even birds and some animals feed on you, especially when you are ripe, and here you are complaining?" shouted Miss Lime. "Do you think I like to be by myself? Sometimes, I wish I could be somebody else. People squint their eyes and wiggle their tongue when they taste me. Boy, am I sour to the taste! People have to squish and crush me ever so hard to extract my juice. At least you Miss Banana do change into a bright yellow when you are ripe, but me, I am forever green in colour, even when I am ripe!"

On hearing this, Miss Watermelon bellowed. "Keep on complaining you idiots! You don't have to lie on your tummy from birth and wake up every morning in the same spot day after day with an ever-expanding abdomen, no matter how little mother earth feeds you. Do you know how uncomfortable I feel just lying there on the ground unable to move? Don't you think I would have much preferred to dangle from a tree where I could enjoy the full warmth of mother sunshine and fresh breeze blowing all around me!"

"Be quiet!" shouted Miss Pear, "Do you have to put up with the cold of winter, a wet spring, a hot summer and a muggy and sombre fall. Do you have to be treated annually with dormant oil and sulphur baths and sprayed continuously with insecticides, so that your children wouldn't be attacked by fungi or bored by worms? Surely I would much rather be a simple citrus fruit like an orange or a grapefruit that live in tropical climate, but here I have been for centuries, and as long as my ancestors and I can recall, we have always been pears. My family and I have never evolved into anything other than what we are."

Miss Orange, who had heard her name mentioned was about to enter the fray, when Mr. Cactus, one of the judges-in-chief who was patiently listening to this ranting, raised his gavel and struck the table with a loud bang! "Enough! Enough! Please stop the bickering!" He ordered at the top of his voice. "You have been created as you are, and your stock will improve if you grow in fertile soil, have favorable growing conditions, receive proper care and be allowed to develop in an atmosphere free of pollutants for which human beings have been fully responsible. Can't you see! We were created from the beginning as we are. Now let's get on with the debate."

Not to be denied an opportunity to voice his opinion, Mr. Lichen whose podium rose high above the others so everyone could have an unrestricted view of him, spoke in a clear but commanding voice. "Is there anyone present among you willing to trade your native place with mine, please speak now, or forever hold your tongue." A hushed silence came over the whole assembly of plants and quieted the atmosphere in the room. Then in a firm voice, but with a solemn tone, Mr. Lichen added. "It is just as I had expected, for not one of you would survive an hour in my extremely cold, harsh and inhospitable environment."

He continued, "Now, therefore, tell me why are you complaining? Don't you think that my ancestors would have preferred to evolve into one of you, who enjoy a hospitable climate year round? My friends, I was created the way I am to live and enjoy my life contentedly in the harshest and most inhospitable environment. God willed it and so it ought to be, and God is infinite in all perfection! And may it please you to know that I live a peaceful and contented life, for very few animals or human beings interrupt my earthly existence." Having expressed himself so eloquently, the other judges mutually agreed to allow the debate to begin.

It was indeed a sad day for a number of plants that never advanced beyond their first round. However, plant species in category 'A'-Miss Apple, Miss Peach, and Miss Grape advanced to the semi-finals.

One by one they began to address the judges in turn. The first qualifier was Miss Peach. After her initial, formal address to the judges, she began "tooting her horn." She boasted that she ripened with a most cheerful and colourful complexion, sometimes bright red, orange or yellow. On hearing this, Miss Apple couldn't contain herself. "Very well," said she, "have you ever looked at me and my family closely? We too ripe in varying colours, sometimes bright green, or pale green, or prime red, or dark red, and even golden."

Mr. Lichen interrupted, "Please Miss Apple you will have your turn to speak, do let Miss Peach continue. Miss Peach, please go on."
"Thank you Sir," said Miss Peach and she continued, "Oh how sweet and tender to the taste are we when fully ripe! We are simply delicious and oh, so pulpy and full of juice."
At the sound of the word juice, Miss Grape interjected. "Oh yea!" she said, "We too come in several varieties just as you Miss Peach, and Miss Apple.

But as far as juice is concerned, neither of you can rival me. I produce the finest juice, which can be drunk pure or be fermented into the finest wines world-wide."

"Mr. Judge, may I please continue?" pleaded Miss Peach.

"Most certainly," Mr. Lichen replied, "but we don't want this debate to last forever, so please confine your submission to the other uses to which you can be put."

"Yes, Sir," she replied politely. "Sir Judges, I can be made into peach ice-cream, peach pie, peach cocktail and jams, or be put in salads, or on waffles, and be stewed or eaten directly off the tree."

"Thank you Miss Peach, said one of the judges, "and now may we please hear from Miss Apple."

Miss Apple stood up and in a commanding voice began to address the assembly. "Learned judges, I can be eaten when still green or when fully ripe. I can be stewed, put in salads, squeezed into juice, made into apple sauce, apple strudel, apple pie, apple cider, and apple cider vinegar." Miss

Apple ended her submission by saying, "My uses are limited only by the inventiveness of the user, Sir Judges."

"Miss Grape, it's your turn," said one of the judges, "What have you to say?"
Miss Grape began by addressing the judges as follows: " Worthy Judges, I stand before you as the mother of all vines. We grapes can be eaten off the vine when ripe. We can be pressed into grape juice, put into salads, especially fruit salads, and most importantly our juice can be fermented into exquisite wines. Some of my families come in varieties that are seedless, so no one needs to worry about pits. We can even withstand freezing and can be picked frozen and made into an expensive but delicious ice wine, which neither Miss Peach nor Miss Apple can hope to emulate. Many people love to have a drink of wine before dinner."

At the conclusion of her submission, the judge for temperate regions interjected, "I guess each of you can be eaten off your tree or vine."
"Yes!" was the response from Miss Peach, Miss Apple and Miss Grape in unison.

The judge continued, "But you Miss Peach, you do have a fuzz on your skin, which must be washed off, and a rather large stone in your stomach.
"Yes I do," said Miss Peach, "but these can be taken care of prior to my being eaten or used."

Mr. Lichen, one of the Judges-in-chief added, "You Miss Grape, you are a great berry and you are famous world-wide for your by-products. Unfortunately many people have become intoxicated by consuming too much of your wines, because of their alcoholic content, furthermore, small children are not allowed to drink alcohol, which puts a limit on your uses to all human beings." Turning his attention to Miss Peach, he continued, "In many ways Miss Peach, you are like Miss Apple, but you have fuzz on your skin, and such a large stone in your stomach. In summary, given these less-than-desirable qualities of Miss Grape and Miss Peach, I have to give the nod to Miss Apple. She would represent fruit trees in temperate regions."

Neither Miss Peach nor Miss Grape was pleased with the decision and plainly showed their disappointment, but knowing that the judges' decision was final, they had no alternative but to accept it.

Attention was then turned to Group B participants from the tropical regions. Mr. Cactus who had witnessed the heated exchanges among the members of the temperate region had long decided that he would have none of this in his segment of the debate and quickly took charge of the proceedings.

Miss Mango was invited to present her case, which she promptly did. She proclaimed herself queen of tropical fruits. She was undeniably beautiful as some of her siblings had a rosy complexion. In her presentation, she explained to the judges that she came in various hues, shapes and sizes and came in several varieties, each sweet to the taste, when ripe. She boasted that she could be eaten when green, semi-ripe and fully ripe, and that she was juicy. Her by-products were many and range from mango chutney to mango ice cream. Her fruit could be curried, stewed, put into fruit salads, made into jams or squeezed into a rich juice.

After Miss Mango had finished giving an account of her attributes, Miss Pineapple danced on her spiny limbs and she too began to enumerate her many fine qualities. She boasted about her famous pineapple slices, so sweet to the taste, her pineapple juice, pineapple tarts, pineapple cakes including the famous pineapple box cake. She boasted that her slices can be used in pizza topping, fruit salad, and meat stew and used to embellish exotic drinks like pina colada and the like. At this juncture, Mr. Cactus interrupted and said, "Now Miss Pineapple, so far so good, but tell us what use can be made of your leaves, and other parts of your body." There was silence. "Miss Pineapple, your leaves can be a source of danger to children or people who are not very careful. Your sharp, serrated edges can be the cause of scrapes, cuts and wounds, can they not?" asked Mr. Cactus. Miss Pineapple sheepishly admitted to this fact.

Following Miss Pineapple's submission, Miss Guava, Miss Kiwi fruit, and Miss Passion Fruit offered their arguments in succession, in order to capture the crown, but the judges were not very impressed with their limited usage, and did not seem very thrilled with their submissions either.

As it was getting late, there was a call for one final submission. One of the judges said, "Before we tally the scores and declare a winner for Tropical regions, we can accommodate one last presentation. Miss Coconut hurriedly advanced to the podium. She bowed and addressed the assembly in the following manner: "Oh wise judges, and you, Sir Chief Judge, kindly hear me out."

Miss Mango, Miss Pineapple, Miss Golden apple and Miss Star apple all came to rapt attention and wondered what Miss Coconut could possibly offer that they couldn't, she who had a very hard outer shell and was not as sweet tasting as they.

Then Miss Coconut dramatically began to address the assembly. "Honorable judges, I stand before you as the 'Queen of Palms." Focussing her attention directly on the Judge-in-chief, she said: "Sir Cactus, I come here to challenge every tropical plant, for there is none who can rival me. Every fibre of my being can be used by humankind. Trust me Sir!" The judges and the whole assembly came to rapt attention.

She continued, "You see brothers and sisters, every part of my fruit can be used when young, not quite ripe or fully ripe. I produce the most relaxing and refreshing, natural drink, coconut water, and no one has to squeeze me to extract this pure wholesome drink. Can you name anyone who does not like to have a cool drink of coconut water? My flesh called jelly, when I am young, can be eaten when soft, medium-hard or hard."

"On maturing into a ripe old age, with wrinkles on my skin, my outer coat can be used as fuel, or burnt to keep mosquitoes away. It can be pounded into fibres to make mattresses, pillows, or cobweb brooms. Do you realize how many people have found comfort while sleeping on fibre mattresses with matching fibre pillows?

Honorable judges, my fully matured kernel can be grated and squeezed to extract its milk, which enriches and add quality flavour to cooked foods. The grated kernel can also be made into coconut cakes, coconut bakes, coconut bread and sugar cakes. Indeed Sirs, even when all the milk has been extracted from my grated kernel, the moist residue can then be fed to swine or chicken, which provide meat for human consumption. My aged kernel when dried and baked by the sun can be transformed into copra, which when pressed, produces cooking oil, and the residue can be made into fertilizer. Good Sirs, do you know how many cooking dishes rely on my oils. In fact, no part of my kernel is wasted!

My inner shell, which protects my flesh and stores my water, though hard and durable can be fashioned into beautiful ornamental designs, or made into musical instruments like the maracas. My inner shell can be cut into halves and made into dipping or drinking cups."

The stems of my fronds can be shaped into cricket bats for use by youngsters in playing the game of cricket. My leaves can be used to tatch roofs, and have sheltered many people from drenching rains. The flexible rib in my leaves which runs through the middle of each leaflet can be made into yard brooms, or used in the construction of kites and bird cages. The shredded leaflets can be woven into baskets, straw hats, belts, purses and the like. My very tree trunk can be sawn and converted into seats. Sirs, I have witnessed the poor making use of my fibrous roots and using them in place of tooth brushes. People would chew on a piece of one of my roots and cleanse their teeth; even birds and insects have feasted on my baby flowers. Need I say more?

Honorable judges, ladies and gentleman, I rest my case."

There was a spontaneous and thunderous ovation from the entire assembly as the place erupted into a prolonged applause. Even Miss Apple, the first place winner in category "A," approached Miss Coconut, and gracefully bowed before her and addressed her in the following words, "You are indeed the queen of our species, for you are truly the greatest food producing plant species, and most valuable asset to human beings. There is no fruit tree, berry or vine plant in any part of the world that can rival the rich and wide variety of your contributions to the well-being of humans. You are indeed worthy of the top award."

All the judges were decidedly unanimous in their approval of Miss Coconut being acclaimed queen of plants, and they congratulated her profusely. On hearing this outpouring of accolades from the judges and from Miss Apple, her chief rival, Miss Coconut acted very humbly and was very accommodating in her acceptance speech.

She addressed them in the following words, "My dear brothers and sisters, please do not praise me, for my existence and my usefulness to human beings come from the Creator, God. He alone created the heavens and the earth and all that's within it."

"With his very own caring hands he made us all, and it is to his credit that he created such variety in our wonderful world: in humans, animals and in plants. Indeed it is He who provided me with all these wonderful gifts. He expects that they would be put to great use, and so it is my pleasure to share them with those who care to use them. And you Miss Apple, Miss Peach, Miss Grape, Miss Pineapple, Miss Mango, Miss Orange, Miss Grapefruit and Miss Passion fruit, and indeed everyone here present including you Mr.

Lichen and Mr. Cactus, you too are useful and beautiful in the eyes of God, for God never makes junk! Everything He has created is good in His eyes, until it is misused or abused."

The judges in Chief, Mr. Lichen and Mr. Cactus and all the other presiding judicial advisors stood, applauded and gave her a prolonged standing ovation. Mr. Cactus spoke and said, "I speak for all of us when I say: Very beautifully expressed, Miss Coconut. Forever will your fronds wave majestically in the breeze, as you stretch upward towards the sky. May you forever stand tall, my friend, as you deserve to be recognized by all as Queen of plant species, and may you enjoy an everlasting reign."

Rising from their seats, the judges proclaimed the Great Debate over. One by one, all the plants returned to their local environment, and to their homes contented to savour the lessons, which they had been taught, and which were so ably propounded by Mr. Lichen and Miss Coconut.